MW00879947

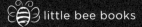 little bee books

251 Park Avenue South, New York, NY 10010
Copyright © 2019 by Little Bee Books
All rights reserved, including the right of
reproduction in whole or in part in any form.

Manufactured in China TPL 0819
ISBN: 978-1-4998-0999-2
First Edition 10 9 8 7 6 5 4 3 2 1

littlebeebooks.com

ISLE OF MISFITS

4 BOOKS IN 1!

#1
FIRST CLASS

#2
THE MISSING POT OF GOLD

#3
PRANK WARS!

#4
THE CANDY CANE CULPRIT

by JAMIE MAE
illustrated by FREYA HARTAS

little bee books

FIRST CLASS

THE MISSING POT OF GOLD

PRANK WARS!

THE CANDY CANE CULPRIT

BOOK 1

Isle of MISFITS
FIRST CLASS

by JAMIE MAE   illustrated by FREYA HARTAS

ISLE OF MISFITS

The Great Castle

THE MAINLAND

The Big City

Gibbon's Castle

The Little Town

CONTENTS

CHAPTER ONE

THE LONELIEST GARGOYLE

Gibbon the gargoyle lived atop the same castle all his life. Gargoyles were meant to protect the buildings they lived on. Sometimes, that meant protecting the people inside those buildings, too. That's what Gibbon was always taught.

But Gibbon couldn't stay still in one place *all* day. Sure, it was what he was *supposed* to do, but it was boring! So Gibbon found something new to do to pass the time: playing pranks on people as they walked by below.

And winter was his favorite season for pranks. Winter meant snowballs.

One snowy day, he saw a man in a suit hurrying by the castle. Gibbon quickly made a snowball in his hands. He held it over the edge and dropped it, watching as it hit the man right on the head.

The man jumped from the shock of the cold snow. A confused look crossed his face when he didn't see anyone around. Holding back laughter, Gibbon rolled another snowball and dropped it on the man. This time, the man yelped and ran off.

"*Gibbon!*" a voice whispered harshly.

He jumped and turned toward the gargoyle speaking to him. Elroy was the leader of the castle gargoyles and almost never broke his silence.

"That's enough," Elroy ordered. "You are too old to be playing pranks on the humans. You need to start taking your post seriously."

"But it's so boring!" Gibbon protested. "We just stand around all day. Even at night, we do nothing! What are we even defending the castle from anyway?"

Elroy did not move, but his eyes glared over at Gibbon. "You need to learn how to work with your team, Gibbon. Your slacking off only makes it harder for the rest of us."

With a sigh, Gibbon looked down at the street. He watched as a group of kids stopped below the castle. One of them picked up some snow and threw it at another. Instead of getting mad, the other kid started laughing and made his own snowball. In no time at all, the kids were in a full-fledged snowball fight!

That's what I want, Gibbon thought. For a very long time, Gibbon watched people's lives from the top of the castle. A lot of them had friends and family and fun, but Gibbon didn't really have any of that. The other gargoyles never wanted to play or laugh. They only wanted to watch the world as it went by.

Maybe if I can get Elroy to play, everyone else will loosen up! he thought.

Gibbon smiled. "Hey, Elroy. Catch me if you can! If you do, I'll sit still and guard the castle the rest of the day!"

With a laugh, Gibbon took off. He climbed down the side of the castle, then darted down an empty street.

Gibbon knew—he just *knew*—if Elroy played with him, he'd understand.

But when he stopped and looked back, he didn't see Elroy. His heart sank.

CHAPTER TWO

DOWN IN THE STREETS

Gibbon stopped walking. Should he go back to the castle? Should he wait a little longer and see if Elroy would follow him?

But the longer Gibbon waited, the more certain he was that Elroy wasn't coming. He hung his head as he started to slink back toward the castle.

Wait a minute, he thought as he stopped and looked around again. *This is the first time I've been off the castle!*

He'd only seen the streets from high above. This was the first time he had come down and walked upon them. Should he really go back?

When he turned around, a man was standing in front of him . . . the same one he had thrown snowballs at earlier!

When Gibbon was up on the castle, humans all looked so *small*, but down on their level, these humans weren't small at all. He was big. Really big!

The man screamed and pointed at Gibbon. "*Wh-what is that?!*"

With a scream of his own, Gibbon ran away. After turning down another, quieter street, Gibbon looked over his shoulder and saw that he was alone. This time, he was glad he wasn't being chased. He slowed down and leaned against a storefront to catch his breath.

Did that human think Gibbon was scary? No way, the human was the scary thing!

I need to get back to the castle, Gibbon thought. There, he could look down at the humans from a safe distance. But when Gibbon glanced around, he didn't know where he was. Having lived his whole life at the castle, he didn't know his way around anyplace else.

Gibbon spun around, hoping to see the castle's towers. When he looked toward the storefront again, he yelled. There was something inside the store staring *right back at him*!

He ran to hide behind a mailbox. He slowly peeked out to see if it was gone. But it wasn't. He saw it again, and this time it was hiding behind a . . . mailbox?

Wait, that can't be right. Gibbon narrowed his eyes at the creature in the window.

He held out a hand and shook it. The creature in the window did the same thing. It was gray and made of stone with two horns coming out of its head. One of its horns was broken in half.

Slowly, he walked out from behind the mailbox. And so did the creature. He walked straight up to it. He was so close, nearly touching it, when . . . *BAM!* He walked right into an invisible wall.

Wait! That's me!

Gibbon frowned as he reached out to touch his half-broken horn. How long had it been like that? Was this really what he looked like? The more he looked at his reflection, the more he realized he didn't much look like the other gargoyles. They were bigger than him, and they all had two full horns.

A sinking feeling formed in Gibbon's chest. He didn't just feel different from the others on the *inside*, he also looked different than them on the *outside*, too.

Even if he looked and felt different, the castle was still the only home he had. When he looked up again to try to find the castle's towers, he stopped. Three gargoyles stood in his path. *Big* gargoyles— even bigger than Elroy.

"Hello, Gibbon. I'm Fitzgerald," the one in the middle said. This gargoyle looked way different than the ones from the castle. He had batlike ears and instead of horns, he had two fangs that curled out of his top lip. And he was HUGE!

"Um, hi?" Gibbon replied curiously. He didn't know there were other gargoyles in the city. Maybe they wanted to be friends? Maybe he could go back to their castle instead of his!

"You've got some explaining to do," Fitzgerald said. "A gargoyle should never leave their post. And a gargoyle should never be seen by humans."

"I didn't mean for the human to see me!" Gibbon groaned. "I was trying to get back to my castle, but I don't know which way it is."

"Oh, Gibbon. You aren't going back to that castle," Fitzgerald said with a chuckle. "We have the perfect place for a restless creature like you."

—— CHAPTER THREE ——
ISLE OF MISFITS

The other two gargoyles grabbed Gibbon's arms. Gibbon tried to twist his way out of their grasp, but they were too strong. The next thing he knew, they were all up in the air. They flew high above the city, weaving between skyscrapers.

"Where are we going?" Gibbon asked. Fitzgerald looked at Gibbon with a sly smile, but didn't answer.

Was he really in a lot of trouble? Who were these gargoyles? Gibbon felt nervous as they flew out of the city.

From the castle's towers, he could sometimes see the shine of the ocean far away, but this was the first time he was seeing it up close. He watched the waves as the gargolyes flew farther and farther away from land. From his home.

Where could they be going?

After flying all night, Gibbon finally spotted a stretch of land over the horizon. As they flew closer, he saw that the island was shaped like a jelly bean and it contained mountains, a lush forest, and a mishmash of buildings. The buildings circled around a grand castle. It was even bigger than the castle Gibbon had lived on.

"That's home," Fitzgerald said as they turned with the wind and flew down.

Once they landed, the two other gargoyles took off toward the castle. "Our castle was the first building on the island. We have protected it, and the island, for a very long time, but after a while we started to get restless. Like you." Fitzgerald explained.

"What *is* this place?" Gibbon asked.

"We call it the Isle of Misfits," Fitzgerald said. "When we started traveling the world, we saw we weren't alone in our curiosity. Many other restless creatures were misbehaving and revealing themselves to people and causing problems. So we decided to turn our island into a place for these misfits, where they can be safe and learn how to be proper monsters. And protectors."

"So, I'm a misfit?" Gibbon asked. His attention drifted from Fitzgerald to two nearby buildings. They were made of wood and had a lot of windows on them. It looked like the top of each building had a garden. Vines wrapped around the sides of the buildings.

"Yes, you are. I've heard about you and your pranks. Once you left your post at the castle, I knew we had to bring you here. You will learn our rules and how to uphold them. One of the most important rules is: *Never be seen by humans*. You've already broken that rule, Gibbon."

Gibbon fidgeted and looked away. "But I didn't know it was a rule!"

"That's why you're here. We'll teach you all there is to know."

"What happens when I learn all the rules? Do I get to go home?"

"If you want. Or you could stay here and go on missions to help other monsters," Fitzgerald said. He waved his hand out toward the rest of the island. "There is a lot to see here. I think you'll like it."

Gibbon looked past Fitzgerald and saw a group of monsters burst out of an old stone building. They were carrying books and backpacks as they walked out of the building. There were so many different kinds of monsters, Gibbon could hardly believe his eyes!

He had only ever seen other gargoyles, but on nights when he had crept into the castle library, he read books about other types of monsters and pored over the pages with pictures, not knowing if they were even real.

Some of the students were in groups, laughing together. Maybe . . . maybe Gibbon could find friends here? At the thought of it, he got so excited, he couldn't stay still.

"I'll give you a tour," Fitzgerald said. He pointed to the smaller buildlings first. "These are where most of your classes will be held. And over there," he pointed toward the wooden buildings with the gardens on top, "are the dorms."

Gibbon nodded eagerly. Near the dorms, he saw a green troll, a hairy gremlin, a slimy ghoul, and a baba yaga, all laughing at a griffin. The griffin was trying to fly, but each time it took off, it veered side to side before falling back down to the ground. It made them laugh even louder.

At first, Gibbon thought it was funny, too. But when he saw how sad the griffin looked, he realized the griffin wasn't playing a game. The griffin really couldn't fly and the others were making fun of it. He was about to go over and say something when Fitzgerald placed a hand on his shoulder.

"Come on, Gibbon," Fitzgerald said. "I'll show you to your dorm room. Tomorrow, you start class."

Inside the dorm, it was bright and airy from all the open windows. A staircase wound up, leading to floor after floor of rooms. As they walked up the staircase, a tiny, sparkly thing flew past Gibbon's head.

"Whoa! Please watch where you're flying, Fiona!" Fitzgerald called out.

"Sorry, boss!" Fiona shouted back.

"What was that?" Gibbon asked as they stopped on the third floor.

"A fairy. I know it might seem overwhelming right now, but you'll adjust. Ah, here is your room! I'll leave you to get settled in," Fitzgerald said as they arrived at a door.

When Fitzgerald opened the door, Gibbon rushed through.

Speechless, he waved goodbye to Fitzgerald before turning his attention back to the room, which had two of everything: two bookcases, two desks, two beds.

"Hi!" came a voice. He turned and saw a dragon who was almost too tall for the room. As the dragon came over, he ran into a dresser and then right into a bed. Gibbon cringed as a shiny red box was knocked off one of the desks and popped open. Gems fell out of the box and spilled everywhere.

"Oops! My treasure!" The dragon bent down to pick them up, but kicked a few away instead.

What a clumsy dragon, Gibbon thought. He knelt down to pick up the shiny rocks that had rolled closer to him and handed them to the dragon.

"Thanks!" the dragon said. "I'm Alistair."

"I'm Gibbon." In comparison to Alistair, Gibbon felt really tiny. As tiny as the fairy that flew by him on the staircase.

Alistair piled his things on the desk before holding out his claw for Gibbon to shake.

Gibbon eyed his claws—they were sharp and long—and wasn't sure if he wanted to touch them.

Alistair frowned and let his arm drop to his side. "I haven't had a roommate all year. I'm happy to have you! It's been a little lonely. Hey, do you want to go to the cafeteria? It's pizza night!"

"Sorry, I'm really tired," Gibbon said as he went over to the open bed.

The island was filled with so many different types of monsters Gibbon had never seen before and it seemed crazy that now he was going to school with all of them.

After traveling all night, the tiredness and shock finally caught up to Gibbon. He just wanted to rest so he could think all of this through.

He could make friends tomorrow, Gibbon decided. Today, he needed to sleep and prepare for his new life on the island.

CHAPTER FOUR

FIRST CLASS

The next day, Gibbon woke to a loud noise. Alistair sat among a pile of books and schedules.

"Sorry! Fitzgerald sent these over while you were sleeping," Alistair explained.

"Thanks," Gibbon said as he picked up a schedule with his name on it and looked it over. On the back, there was a map of the island with each of the buildings marked so he would know where to go.

"We're in the same first class, so I'll show you where it is. It's out in the field where we have all our PE classes. Let's go, we're gonna be late!"

Gibbon tumbled out of bed. He didn't want to be late on his very first day! They gathered up their school books and rushed out of the dorm.

Alistair led Gibbon to a big field in the center of the island. Objects were all around the field, kind of like a maze, but Gibbon wasn't sure what they were for.

"Welcome to PE," the teacher said. Because they got to class late, they were in the very back. It was hard for Gibbon to see over all the creatures in front of him.

"I'm Mr. Dimas and I will be your teacher this year." Gibbon didn't understand why Mr. Dimas was a teacher here. He looked like a normal human. That was until he started walking and Gibbon saw the bottom half of him—he was half horse! *A centaur*, Gibbon realized. He had read about them, but never seen a real, live one. *Wow!*

"For our first class, we'll be working on an obstacle course. It's important to learn how to think fast and work with a team. Everyone, get into groups!" Mr. Dimas ordered.

"Did you see that? He's a centaur!" Gibbon turned toward Alistair, but Alistair was gone. Everyone had quickly gathered into groups. Now he was the only one standing by himself.

Everyone else already has friends, I guess, he thought sadly. The group closest to him looked familiar. It took him a minute to remember they had been the ones laughing at the griffin yesterday. Maybe they weren't actually mean?

He decided to be brave and go say hello. "Hi, I'm Gibbon! Today's my first day here."

The hairy gremlin looked over and narrowed her eyes. "So?"

"Look at his broken horn!" the ghoul said with a laugh.

The troll squinted its eyes. "And you're so small."

"Go away, tiny gargoyle," the baba yaga said.

They laughed at Gibbon as he walked away with his tail dragging behind him. Even surrounded by other monsters, Gibbon still felt alone.

"Why don't you join us?" someone said. Gibbon looked up to see a yeti with so much hair, Gibbon couldn't see his face.

"I'm Yuri," the yeti said. "We could use one more monster."

"Thanks!" Gibbon said as he looked at the rest of the group. Alistair was there, along with the griffin that couldn't fly, and a very angry-looking fairy.

―――― CHAPTER FIVE ――――

ON YOUR MARK, GET SET, GO!

Gibbon didn't think the obstacle course looked too hard. There was a net to crawl under and a tree to climb up, followed by a tall wall to scale using a rope, a series of poles to maneuver through, and at the very end, a track to sprint down to get to the flag.

"The first team to grab the flag wins," Mr. Dimas explained after he walked the groups through the obstacle course. "Now, everyone decide which team member will do each part of the course."

"We should introduce ourselves. I'm Ebony," the griffin said to Gibbon. Her voice was soft and nice.

"You know me already."
Alistair smiled and gave
Gibbon a thumbs-up.

"Fiona," the fairy muttered.

Gibbon was surprised. She
was small and sparkly, so he
had expected a happier voice
to come out of her. Instead,
she sounded grumpy and
had a serious frown
on her face.

"Who are those guys?" Gibbon asked as he nodded toward the other group. The baba yaga barked orders to her teammates, telling each of them where to go.

"Don't mess it up!" the baba yaga ordered. "We have to win!"

"They're . . . not very nice," Alistair said.

Yuri nodded. "Avoid them if you can."

"They're the top students in our class. Always get the highest grades on tests. Always winning competitions," Ebony said with a sigh.

"Won't be winning any personality contests, though," Fiona added.

Gibbon chuckled. He had a feeling he was really going to like it here.

Gibbon was up first. He was so excited to show the team what he could do.

"On your marks, get set, *go*!" called out Mr. Dimas.

The first obstacle was the net that had to be crawled under. He got on his belly and started to crawl and the grumpy ghoul next to him did the same. Gibbon was almost the first one finished when one of his horns got caught in the net.

"Argh!" Gibbon cried out as he struggled to break free. The ghoul laughed at him as he slid out from under the net.

Gibbon finally broke free. Embarrassed, he ran to the tree. He had to make up for that!

"What are you doing? *I'm* supposed to be next!" Alistair called out after him.

Instead of tagging Alistair's hand, he jumped off the ground and flew quickly up the tree as the hairy gremlin was weaving her way up. The gremlin was very fast and Gibbon couldn't catch up to her.

She got to the top first, freeing the rope and throwing it down to the baba yaga.

No! Gibbon finally made it to the top. He started to fly over to the next obstacle, the wall.

"No flying over the wall, you have to climb it with the rope!" Mr. Dimas called out to Gibbon.

Gibbon circled back to the rope in the tree, using it to climb over the wall.

"Wait, you were supposed to give it to me!" Yuri shouted.

"It's okay, I can do this!" he said to Yuri.

Gibbon looked around to see how the other teams were doing. He was shocked. Almost *all* the other teams were ahead of him now. What would happen if he came in last? Would everyone hate him?

I'll have no friends! I can't let that happen!

The next part of the obstacle course was a real challenge. He had to be quick and careful.

As much as he tried to avoid them, he bumped into nearly all the poles as he went through. By the time he got out, the flag at the end of the track was gone.

The troll was holding the flag. His team was laughing and patting each other on the backs as the rest of the students gathered around to cheer them on. When they saw Gibbon, the ghoul grinned and pointed right at him.

"Loser," he said.

Gibbon walked back to his team with his head down. He was so sure he'd win. When he looked up, he saw them glaring at him.

"What was that? We're supposed to work together," Fiona snapped. "Now, we lost!"

"That wasn't cool, Gibbon," Ebony said.

Yuri and Alistair only shook their heads as they left.

— CHAPTER SIX —

A DIFFERENT KIND OF OBSTACLE

Alistair ignored Gibbon all night. He even left for class all week without him. It made Gibbon feel even more alone to walk to class by himself.

"Hey, little guy," the baba yaga said. Gibbon turned around to see the slimy ghoul with the baba yaga. "We were never introduced. I'm Lissa."

"And I'm Gashsnarl," the ghoul said.

"Hello. I'm uh, Gibbon," the gargoyle responded.

"Did you hear about the obstacle course challenge at the end of the week?" Gashsnarl said. "The team that wins gets their very own mission."

"That's right! But don't get your hopes up. We're going to win." Lissa said with a big grin.

"Yeah, we always win," Gashsnarl said, high-fiving Lissa.

"You and your friends shouldn't even bother trying," Lissa said.

"That's not true! We're going to win, just wait and see!" Gibbon declared.

Now all he had to do was convince them that he could be a team player.

Gibbon had to find the others. This would be the perfect way to make up for his mistake earlier. This time they'd do it together, as a team. And they'd win. Maybe once they won, they wouldn't be mad at him anymore.

And they would get to go on a mission! Going on a mission meant he could see the world—he'd see more than just his castle and the island. *Not only that, but see the world with friends*, Gibbon thought. Nothing would be more fun than that!

He found them at a table in the corner
of the cafeteria.

"Hey, guys," he said nervously.

Yuri moved so that he took up the rest
of the bench, leaving no room for Gibbon

"We lost because of him," Yuri said.

"We didn't just lose," Fiona added, "we
came in *last* place!"

"I'm really sorry about doing the course myself, guys," Gibbon said. "I thought if I did well, you guys would want to be my friends. I guess . . . I'm not very good at working on a team. Back home, no one ever wanted to do anything with me, so I was always by myself. I know I messed up yesterday. I'm really sorry."

"You didn't have to win all by yourself to become our friend," Ebony said.

"Yeah, *seriously*. If you wanted to be friends, all you had to do was ask. Duh!" Fiona shook her head.

"Really?" Gibbon asked, surprised. "That's all it would take?"

Yuri scooted over so Gibbon could sit down with them.

"Did you guys hear about the obstacle course challenge next month?" Gibbon asked.

"Of course. We already signed up for it," Alistair said.

"Oh," Gibbon mumbled.

"Why should we let you back on our team?" Yuri asked. "How do we know you won't pull the same stunt as yesterday?"

Gibbon frowned. "I've never really been part of a team before. But I get it now. How we have to work together. Can I . . . can I *please* be a part of your team? Please?"

Ebony looked at her friends. "He said 'please.'"

Alistair sighed. "It's not easy being new here, guys."

Yuri nodded.

Fiona rolled her eyes, but nodded, too.

CHAPTER SEVEN

A SECOND CHANCE

Every day after school for weeks, the five of them trained on the practice course. Yuri was good at deciding what obstacle each of them would do best with the skill they had, even though his hair kept him from seeing very well.

"Why don't you tie your hair up?" Gibbon suggested. "I've seen the really hairy humans do it! I think they call it a 'man bun'?"

"I think it's a good idea! I have some ribbon." Ebony pulled a blue ribbon off her backpack and handed it to Yuri.

"If you guys are sure," Yuri said uncertainly. He tied his hair up into a bun. It was the first time Gibbon could see his eyes—they were ice blue. "Wow! This does make a big difference!"

"Are you guys ready for the challenge?" Alistair asked as he landed next to them. "It's almost time, we should head over."

Everyone nodded. But as soon as they got there, Gibbon's heart sank. The obstacle course looked completely different than the practice one! They had spent all that time training for nothing.

"Uh-oh! It's not the same!" Ebony fluttered her wings in a panic.

"Oh, great, just great," Fiona grunted.

"Let's stay calm, guys," Yuri said.

Unlike the last course, this one started with a tube you had to crawl through. Then there was a seesaw that you had to carefully walk across. After that, there were zigzag balance beams over a mud pit. Next, there was a net wall to climb over. Last, there was a fence to jump over before someone could grab the flag.

"This is totally different," Alistair said as he chewed on his claws. "What are we going to do now?"

"I've got an idea," Yuri said as he huddled everyone together. "Okay, so here's the plan. . . ."

"On your marks, get set, *go*!" Mr. Dimas blew his whistle.

Ebony was up first. She couldn't fly very well, but she was great at crawling through tubes. She was out first and slapped Fiona's hand.

Fiona delicately walked across the seesaw. Thanks to how tiny she was, the boards barely moved under her weight, which made it easier for her to keep her balance than the other creatures.

She jumped off the other side and high-fived Yuri.

Carefully, Yuri edged his way along the zigzag balance beams. At the final turn, he wobbled so much, Gibbon thought he was going to fall, but he caught his balance at the last second and high-fived Alistair.

Alistair was nearly as big as the net wall, so scaling it was easy for him. The troll from the other team was close behind!

Alistair jumped down from the wall and high-fived Gibbon.

The gargoyle ran as fast as he could to the fence, then jumped over it.

He only had a small ways to go before he could grab the flag, but he was neck and neck with Lissa.

He was so close! *CRASH!*

Gibbon went tumbling down. He looked up and saw the baba yaga smirking as she grabbed the flag.

No! He sat on the ground and held his head in his hands. *I was so close!*

— CHAPTER EIGHT —
AND THE AWARD GOES TO . . .

They had almost won the race, only to lose at the last second. How could he let this happen?

"What's wrong?" Ebony asked.

"I'm so sorry," Gibbon said. "I lost it for our team."

"Are you kidding me?" Yuri said as he came over. He patted Gibbon on the shoulder. "We came in second!"

"*Second!*" Alistair shouted. "We got *second place*!"

"We've never done that before!" Fiona said. Even she was smiling.

"You're . . . happy?" Gibbon asked as he looked up at the group. "Really?"

"We almost always end up in last place. What's not to be happy about?" Ebony asked with a grin.

Alistair held his claw out to Gibbon. "Come on, friend. It's okay."

Gibbon smiled as he took Alistair's claw and stood up. *Friend*. Gibbon looked from Ebony to Fiona to Yuri, then to Alistair. He had friends.

And that felt even better than winning.

Lissa, Gashsnarl, and the rest of their team stood up on a stage with Mr. Dimas and Fitzgerald. Gibbon wasn't looking forward to watching them gloat.

Mr. Dimas whispered something to Fitzgerald. Fitzgerald nodded and looked out into the crowd.

"Will Alistair, Gibbon, Ebony, Fiona, and Yuri please join us onstage?" Fitzgerald asked.

Gibbon jumped from surprise at hearing his name. He looked to his friends, who also had wide eyes.

"*Us*?" Alistair whispered.

They all walked up onstage together. Gibbon felt awkward being up there with all the other monsters watching him, so he hid halfway behind Alistair, grateful that his roommate was so big.

"What's going on?" the hairy gremlin asked angrily.

"They don't deserve to be up here with us," snapped the troll.

"Of course they do," Fitzgerald replied. "Because *they* are the winners."

"WHAT?!" Lissa shouted.

"I saw you trip Gibbon at the end," Mr. Dimas said to Lissa. "Winners don't cheat. You are hereby disqualified."

The other teams gasped.

"We won?" Ebony said. "Really?"

"Yes, really." Fitzgerald turned to them with a big smile. "I'm very proud of all of you for learning to work so well together. That's exactly why we are here. I'm glad to see you have found some friends, Gibbon."

Gibbon smiled and nodded. He was happy to have friends now and a new place to call home.

"I was going over this mission and well, I think it would be perfect for your team and your . . . unusual set of skills," Fitzgerald said, looking at each of them.

"We get the mission?" Fiona asked.

Fitzgerald smiled. "Only if you want it. So, what do you say? Are you ready?"

They all looked at each other in amazement. "We're ready!"

Isle of

MISFITS

THE MISSING POT OF GOLD

BOOK 2

by JAMIE MAE   illustrated by FREYA HARTAS

CONTENTS

— CHAPTER ONE —

READY TO ROLL

When Gibbon and his friends earned their very first mission to help another creature in trouble, he didn't think it would start with them in a classroom. Wasn't the whole point of going on a mission to get away from the academy? Gibbon tapped his claw against his desk as he waited for the professor to arrive.

Ebony, of course, sat in the very front of the room. She eagerly arranged her colorful pens and notebooks on her desk. Fiona sighed loudly as she fluttered around, filled with too much energy to stay still.

Gibbon sat in the middle, bored as he stared at the clock. Yuri was behind him, snoring away.

Suddenly, the door burst open. Yuri sat up straight and Fiona darted over to her desk as Fitzgerald entered the classroom.

"You've got a great mission!" he announced as he walked in.

Ebony flipped open one of her notebooks and picked up a pen to start taking notes.

"You're going to Ireland," Fitzgerald explained. "You'll be helping a leprechaun by the name of Declan find his missing pot of gold."

"Leprechauns?" Fiona whined. "Seriously?"

Yuri perked up. "What's wrong with leprechauns?"

"Have you ever *met* a leprechaun?" Fiona muttered.

Yuri shook his head, looking at Gibbon and Alistair. Both of them shrugged.

"Just wait," she grumbled. "You'll see what I mean. Or smell, at least."

"Now, now," Fitzgerald said, "a leprechaun's gold is their whole life savings. If you don't find it, he'll have nothing. You'll have to look for clues, decode their meanings, and piece it all together to figure out what happened. Now if you're all ready, follow me."

Gibbon leapt to his feet. Ireland! A whole new adventure with his friends!

When they arrived at the leprechaun village, Gibbon was in awe. It was unlike any place he could have ever imagined. Apparently, leprechauns were tiny little creatures with brightly colored hair and big, booming laughs. They bustled about the town filled with mushroom homes and shops built into trees. He didn't remember much about leprechauns except that they had something to do with being lucky? Or gold? Or maybe something to do with a rainbow?

Fiona grumbled as she waved her hand in front of her nose. "Leprechauns always smell like mud. It's like they bathe in the stuff. *Ugh!* Someone needs to teach them about the wonders of soap and water."

"Oh, hush," Ebony replied. Her big, black eyes scanned the village like it was a treat she couldn't wait to devour.

"Everything's so . . . tiny," Alistair whispered, rubbing his claws against the back of his neck. He was so much larger than everything else around him. One wrong step and he might accidentally stomp someone's home completely flat. Considering how clumsy Alistair was, it was a real risk.

Gibbon knew his friend was clumsy, but it was Fiona he was really worried about. He'd thought she'd be happy to be back in her homeland of Ireland, but he could never really tell what would rub Fiona's fiery temper the wrong way.

"Where do you think Declan lives?" Yuri wondered aloud.

"Declan?" a nearby leprechaun laughed. His friend joined him and they shook their heads over cups of tea they poured out of a mushroom pot. "You mean Scatterbrains? Lost his pot of gold again, did he?"

"Does that happen a lot—hey, what's your name?" Ebony inquired.

115

The leprechaun eyed Ebony, like she was a strange sight. Gibbon guessed that, to them, a griffin probably looked weird. Fiona was the only creature in the group they were used to seeing.

"The name's Rory, and this here is Liam. Declan is a bit . . ." Rory frowned as he stroked his long, green beard.

"Declan's missing a few pieces up here," Liam said, tapping the side of his head. "He's lost his pot of gold four times in just the last year alone. Always forgetting which rainbow he put it under, I tell ya'. It's never *really* lost."

"Give him a week and he'll remember where he put it," said Rory.

"See, Fitz?" Fiona muttered. "He probably just misplaced it or something."

Fitzgerald crossed his arms. "I admit, Declan isn't the most reliable source, but this time he's sure someone took his gold. Your job is to find out what happened and get it back to him."

"We've got this!" Yuri declared as he high-fived Alistair.

Gibbon laughed, but he noticed that Ebony looked uncertain. And Fiona looked downright annoyed.

It'll be okay, he thought. *We're ready!*

THE GOOFBALL

——— GIBBON ———
HEIGHT: 2.2 feet
WEIGHT: 176 pounds
STRENGTH: Optimistic
WEAKNESS: Unable to sit still
BIGGEST FEAR: Humans
FAVORITE FOOD: Candy canes

——— FIONA ———
HEIGHT: 7 inches
WEIGHT: 1.02 pounds
STRENGTH: Cunning
WEAKNESS: Unstable temper
BIGGEST FEAR: None
FAVORITE FOOD: Tears

THE TOUGH ONE

THE BRAINS

——— EBONY ———
HEIGHT: 6 feet, 10 inches
WEIGHT: 399 pounds
STRENGTH: Super-smart
WEAKNESS: Poor flying skills
BIGGEST FEAR: Failing classes
FAVORITE FOOD: Peanut butter
& jelly sandwiches

—— YURI ——
HEIGHT: 8 feet, 2 inches
WEIGHT: 476 pounds
STRENGTH: Tying a man bun
WEAKNESS: Tropical climates
BIGGEST FEAR: Naked mole-rats
FAVORITE FOOD: Artichokes

THE LEADER

THE KLUTZ

—— ALISTAIR ——
HEIGHT: 16 feet
WEIGHT: 1.5 tons
STRENGTH: Fire-breathing
WEAKNESS: Clumsy
BIGGEST FEAR: Knights in
shining armor
FAVORITE FOOD: Anything
charred

THE MISSING
POT OF GOLD

CHAPTER TWO

REALLY SMELLY LEPRECHAUNS

Declan's house was made out of a big, red mushroom located right below an ancient tree. Upon entering it, his home looked like a bomb of clothes and pots went off in it, which made Ebony think the leprechauns in town had been right about Declan. He *was* scatterbrained.

Maybe he really had just put his pot of gold under the wrong rainbow?

Ebony watched as Declan ran around his kitchen, trying to find teacups. He wanted to serve them tea as they talked, but so far, he hadn't been able to find anything but a few pots and pans.

"I know I have cups here somewhere. . . ." Declan muttered to himself.

Yep, completely unorganized, Ebony thought.

"Just tell us what happened already!" Fiona squeaked.

Yuri and Gibbon had sat on the couch in the living room. Yuri had to hunch over to avoid hitting his head on the ceiling. Alistair had to poke his head in through the window since he was far too large to fit inside the mushroom house.

"Right!" Declan closed his kitchen cabinets and turned toward them. "I went to the end of the south rainbow; it's the one that you can see directly over town. I *know* I left my pot of gold there—"

"We were told that you forget which rainbow you leave your gold under all the time," Yuri said. His ice-blue eyes watched Declan.

Good point, Ebony thought. She wished she had brought that up, but she was too nervous to speak. She kept having thoughts like . . . *What if I'm bad at piecing together clues? What if I ask the wrong questions? What if the team would be better off without me?*

"No, this time I *know* I left it under the south rainbow!" Declan declared hotly. "Besides, when I went to check on my gold, the pot was still there. But now, it's empty! You can go and see for yourselves."

"Oh, trust us. We will!" Fiona said. "Do you know how common it is for a leprechaun to leave gold at the end of a rainbow? It's like you were asking for someone to steal it."

Declan frowned. "Where else would I leave my gold then?"

"A secret room in a castle!" Gibbon suggested. "It always worked for me."

"No—a treasure box deep in a cave," Alistair chimed in.

"Those would have been better places," Declan said as his shoulders sagged. His attention shifted up to the ceiling, which was drooping in the center. Between that and the creak of the floorboards, Ebony guessed he needed to do some repairs.

"Don't worry, Declan. We're here to help you," Ebony said.

"Yeah, we'll find it!" Gibbon stood up and placed his hands on his hips like he was a superhero.

Even if she had her doubts about her own abilities, Ebony believed Gibbon. Her team hadn't let her down yet, and she wasn't about to let down Declan, either.

—— CHAPTER THREE ——

WHERE LEPRECHAUNS REALLY HIDE THEIR GOLD

Yuri had suggested that they start by questioning other leprechauns around the village. Alistair was glad to start searching for some real clues.

But none of us know what we're doing, he realized. Yuri liked to pretend he knew the best place to start, but deep down, none of them had ever done this before.

If Ebony had spoken up and said something, Alistair would have believed her without a doubt. She was, after all, the smartest creature in their whole group. Their whole academy even.

But she was following along with their plans, whispering about how she hoped she didn't get anything wrong.

To Alistair, Ireland smelled fresh—like trees and flowers and berries. The leprechauns didn't smell as nice, but since the dragon was by far the biggest creature in the village, his head was closer to the beautiful trees.

None of the leprechauns seemed like they enjoyed having the misfits in their town. The first three leprechauns they tried to talk to ran away. Finally, they came across a leprechaun with bright pink hair. Gibbon asked if she would answer some questions, and she grunted and shrugged in reply.

"That's a yes," Fiona muttered. "Leprechauns aren't wordy."

"Little fairy thinks she knows what's what, does she now?" the pink leprechaun asked, glaring.

"Hey, who are you calling 'little'?" Fiona flew up to the leprechaun. Even compared with these small creatures, Fiona was still super-small. Smaller than Alistair's claws.

He loved his friend, but he also worried that he'd accidentally squash her if he wasn't careful. *It's not always fun being the biggest creature around*, he thought.

"Okay, okay." Yuri stepped between the two fierce girls. "We're sorry, ma'am. Do you know Declan? We're trying to help him find his gold."

The leprechaun sighed and shook her head. "Don't ma'am me, child! Name's Beth. And aye, I heard Declan lost his gold again. Poor fella, this is—what? The fourth time this year?"

"Yeah, we've heard it's happened a few times already," Ebony said sadly.

A big laugh left the leprechaun, bigger and louder than anything Alistair had ever heard. "Oh, it's been a lot more than a few! You know what his biggest problem is?"

"What?" Gibbon asked curiously.

"He still puts it at the end of a rainbow. Can you believe that?"

"Well, where do you keep *your* gold then?" Ebony asked.

"Ha, ha, *ha*, young lassie," Beth said with a firm shake of her head. "I'm not about to tell you that! How do I know you won't go stealing it?"

"We're here to *help* a leprechaun find his missing gold, not take anyone else's," Alistair said.

Beth looked from Ebony back to Alistair with narrowed eyes. "How about this? I'll tell you some places I've heard *other* leprechauns hide their gold?"

"Yes, thank you!" Ebony said.

"One bloke puts his in a hollowed-out tree, though he does have to worry about squirrels getting at it. Another gal hides hers in her gym locker because no one in their right mind would want to go near that awful stench. And a fella I know keeps his buried in his garden. He planted some pretty flowers above it, so he could remember where it was."

With that, Beth wandered off. Maybe Declan *had* left his pot somewhere else and simply forgot. Alistair could sympathize with his situation. He had done that before with some of his things, too. One of the good things about having a roommate was having a friend who could help him find lost things now.

"We should split up," Yuri said. "Ebony and Alistair, you fly to the end of the south rainbow and look for Declan's gold there. The rest of us will search the forest nearby and try to think of other places he might have left his gold—"

"I don't want to go running all around Ireland," Fiona whined.

Yuri sighed, the bun on the top of his head bobbing as he did. "Okay . . . how about you stay with Declan then?"

"That's not what I had in mind," she grumbled.

"Well, you could look around his place while you're there—see if he left his gold somewhere inside the house. How's that sound?"

A smile formed at the edge of her lips. "So, I'd be like a spy?"

Yuri smirked. "Yup! A secret fairy spy."

CHAPTER FOUR

THE FIRST CLUE

Yuri and Gibbon left to explore the forest. It was a little cold in Ireland, but Yuri liked that. He was from a naturally cold climate, and the Isle of Misfits was a little warmer than what he was used to. He missed the snow, so the gray chill in Ireland felt nice.

As they wandered through the forest, he looked at the ground and also at the tops of the trees, trying to find any clues as to where Declan might have hidden his gold. After checking all the bushes and hollowed-out trees they could find, they came up with nothing.

Gibbon kicked a twig on the ground. "How haven't we found any clues?"

Yuri shrugged. This mission wasn't as exciting as he had hoped, but at least they were helping someone. That's what was important.

"I know it's not the most fun," Yuri said, turning to Gibbon. "But we wouldn't be proving ourselves if we fail this mission. And Declan, scatterbrained as he might be, really does need our help."

"I guess you're right," Gibbon said with a sigh.

Together, they kept searching the forest. They walked through an open field and across a stream. Once again, it led to nothing. Maybe Yuri had been wrong about searching the forest?

What would Fitzgerald do in my situation? Gibbon wondered.

"Yuri! Yuri! I found something!"

Yuri jumped up in surprise and ran over to his friend, who held a pot of gold in his hands. He danced around, jiggling the gold as he did. Yuri was ready to start dancing, too! Until he saw the coins. His face fell.

"Wait . . . That isn't Declan's. . . ."

Gibbon frowned and stopped dancing. "How do you know that?"

Yuri reached in and picked up a piece of gold. It had a leprechaun's face on it, but it was a girl! "Leprechauns put their faces on their gold, so they know which is theirs. This isn't Declan's face."

"Oh." Gibbon dropped the pot with a thud.

"Come on, put it back where you found it and let's keep searching." Yuri said.

Just when they were about to give up, they came across a very dark and still lake. It seemed so big, Yuri couldn't see land on the other side of it.

"Let's rest here," Yuri suggested as he sat down and dipped his feet into the lake. Yuri sighed with relief. The chill of the water felt so nice. When Gibbon didn't join him, he looked over to see his friend staring nervously at the water. "What's wrong?"

"I can't swim," Gibbon muttered. "At least, I don't think so. I've never tried. But I'm pretty sure I'd sink to the bottom like a stone. You know, because I *am* stone."

Yuri chuckled and patted the grass beside him. "Don't worry, this is the shallow part of the lake. You could stand in the water here and it'd only come up to your waist!"

Gibbon looked at the water one more time before he slowly walked over and sat down next to Yuri. Once he dipped his feet in, his shoulders relaxed and he smiled. "This isn't so bad."

"Told you so." Yuri grinned.

Something bright in the water caught Yuri's eye. He squinted and looked harder— was he imaging it? No! When the sun broke through the gray clouds, something definitely shimmered in the water.

"Gibbon, do you see that?"

Gibbon looked where Yuri was pointing. "I do!" He stepped down into the water. For a second, he froze like he was too scared to go any farther. But then Gibbon took a half step forward. Then another. With each step, Gibbon looked a little more relaxed. With the water up to his waist, he leaned down and picked up a piece of gold off the bottom of the lake. "Is this Declan?"

Yuri took it from Gibbon and examined it. It was *definitely* Declan's face on the coin. "It is! We've found the gold! Though, uh . . . where's the rest of it?"

Something big moved in the water behind Gibbon. It went by so quickly though, Yuri didn't know if it was a bird's shadow or if there was something else in the water with them.

Yuri looked around, but he didn't see anything else shimmer in the sunlight. If one piece glimmered enough for them to see it through the dark water, he was pretty sure other pieces would've been noticeable, too. "Do you see anything?"

Gibbon glanced around. "Nope. Maybe whoever took the gold only passed through here and dropped one coin?"

"Let's go show this to the others," Yuri suggested. He didn't know what was in the water. Maybe it was just his imagination, but he didn't want to stick around to find out.

— CHAPTER FIVE —

FRIGHTFUL FLYING

Ebony was terrified. Completely terrified. Her whole body shook as she and Alistair walked to the edge of town. Alistair had wanted to take off right away, but she had talked him out of it. She said it would be easier if they got the edge of town first, just to make sure they didn't hit anyone when they flew away.

Truth was, Ebony hated the idea of flying to the end of the rainbow. Who knew how far it would be? What if the rainbow went on forever? Okay, she knew it couldn't go on *forever.* But it could still be a very long flight and she could barely go a few feet without crashing.

"Ready?" Alistair asked with a bright smile.

"Yes?" Ebony hadn't meant her answer to sound like a question, but it did.

"Are you okay?" Alistair tilted his head as he looked closely at her.

"You know how I feel about flying," she whispered. Everyone at the academy had seen her fall at least once, if not a hundred times. She was a laughingstock two years in a row at Flying for Beginners and still dreaded the class.

"I know," Alistair said. "But don't worry. I'll be right here next to you. I'll help you the whole way."

Ebony felt a little better. Alistair had always been good at flying. Maybe he wasn't the most coordinated creature on the ground, but in the air, he was a whole different dragon.

"Come on!" Alistair held out his claw for Ebony's. With a deep breath, she took it and closed her eyes. "On the count of three, okay? One . . . two . . . three!"

With all her might, she flapped her wings and took off. She had barely gotten off the ground when the wind blew so hard that she lost her balance. Ailstair gripped her tighter and helped her steady herself.

"It's okay, you've got this!"

After a few moments, Ebony started to believe him. Maybe she *did* have this!

"You're doing great, Ebony!"

Ebony didn't want to open her eyes. She thought as soon as she did, she'd go crashing down to the ground below. But she also couldn't fly blindly, so she slowly opened one eye at a time.

Though she faltered a few times, Alistair never let her fall. He grabbed her talons tightly to keep her in the air until she caught her balance.

After ten minutes, they came to the end of the rainbow near a lake and landed.

"You did great!" Alistair gave her a nice, though hard, pat on the shoulder.

He definintely doesn't realize his own strength, Ebony thought as she wobbled from the force. She watched her friend, all smiles and laughs, as he looked out across the big lake they landed near.

"Alistair, can I ask you something?"

"Sure."

"How come you're so happy all the time? Others make jokes about your clumsiness and, well, you *are* kind of clumsy."

Alistair laughed again. She'd always admired that. It was one of the reasons she wanted to be friends with him in the first place.

Ebony, on the other hand, was always a little nervous around others. She knew everyone was thinking about how crazy it was that a griffin couldn't fly well.

"You have to focus on the good," Alistair said, looking at the rainbow above them. "Maybe you aren't the best flyer, but you are at the top of our Identifying Monsters and A History of Monstrology courses. You should focus on that—what you're good at—instead of what you're maybe not so good at."

Ebony smiled. "You know something? You're pretty smart, too, Alistair."

"I like to think so," he said with a big grin. "Now, let's look for that pot of gold!"

They searched all along the edge of the lake. The water was murky, so it was hard to see anything more than some rocks and some plants swaying beneath the water. Not long after they started searching, Alistair tripped. For a guy who made flying look easy, he really wasn't that great on the ground.

"Oh, Alistair," Ebony chuckled as she walked over to help him up.

He glanced back at what he had tripped on. "Hey, it's a pot! Do you think this is Declan's?" Alistair asked.

Ebony poked her head into it, but didn't see anything that showed it was Declan's. All she found inside of it was a pool of water and some plants. When Alistair picked it up to examine the plants closer, Ebony noticed that they looked exactly like the ones in the lake.

How strange! she thought.

"Let's look around a little longer," Alistair suggested. They searched the area where the pot was found until something glimmering near the lake caught Ebony's attention. When she went closer, she realized it was a piece of gold . . . with Declan's face on it! "Alistair, come see this!"

"Wow, real gold!" Alistair said. "I don't see any more around, do you?"

Ebony shook her head. "Maybe it's the only piece left behind. We should ask Declan when the last time it rained was. If it was recent, it would explain the water inside the pot. But if not . . . well, I don't know. Let's bring the plants, too, just in case they turn out to be a clue."

Alistair nodded and held out his free claw to her. With a deep breath, she took his claw and jumped up into the air.

CHAPTER SIX

FINDERS KEEPERS

Fiona didn't like being stuck at Declan's. Not. At. All. It smelled like rotting vegetables and the floorboards creaked whenever Declan walked around. Everything was a mess, too. His bed was unmade, his clothes were all over the floor, and his kitchen looked like everything had fallen out of the cabinets.

No wonder he's taking so long to make a cup of tea, she thought as she looked under the bed and inside some of the drawers. She even checked his kitchen cabinets, only to discover that's where Declan kept his toothbrush (and a lawn gnome for some odd reason).

When Fiona's searching turned up no clues, she huffed and sat down. Maybe her friends had found the gold at the end of some other rainbow where Declan had probably left it and forgot, like everyone in town was saying.

If not, Fiona wasn't really sure what to do next. Her friends were some of the smartest creatures at the academy, so she was sure they'd bring back the pot of gold—but should they? If someone came across his gold and took it, she was pretty sure that was within their rights. Finders keepers, after all. Wasn't that a thing with leprechauns' gold?

Declan set a bowl of tea down in front of Fiona, snapping her out of her thoughts. She eyed the bowl and lifted an eyebrow at Declan as she took a sip.

"Sorry, I still can't find any of my cups. I don't know where I put them. . . ."

"Maybe check under the sink in the bathroom," she said. When she had been searching, she was pretty sure she'd seen cups there.

"Oh, I'd never think to look there!" he said with a bright smile.

But apparently you'd think to put them there in the first place, Fiona thought as she took another sip of tea. It wasn't half bad, actually.

"You might have a messy house, Declan, but you sure do know how to make a good cup of tea," she said.

Declan beamed at the compliment. "Thanks! It's an old family recipe, the skin of a mushroom, lavender with a dash of honey, and a hint—only a hint!—of mud for that grit-in-your-mouth texture."

Fiona choked on her next sip. When Declan glanced away, she silently spat the tea back into the bowl.

"I'm sorry about my place," Declan muttered as he looked around. "There was a bad storm two weeks ago and the rain flooded it. I thought I was going to drown, honestly. I was going to get my roof and floors fixed so it doesn't happen again. But I can't pay for any of the repairs I need without my gold."

"Wait, is that why your home looks like this?" Fiona asked. "Because of the flood? We thought you were just sloppy."

Declan nodded. "I know, it's embarrassing . . . but I thought, what's the point in cleaning now? Without fixing the problems, it'll just get messed up when it rains again."

Fiona couldn't help it—she felt sorry for Declan. Maybe he wasn't the most organized creature, but no one deserved for their home to be flooded. She frowned as she looked at the droopy ceiling and mishappen, sticky floorboards.

Maybe finders keepers isn't right, Fiona thought.

CHAPTER SEVEN

THE BIG LIGHTBULB MOMENT

Gibbon and Yuri got back to Declan's place at the same time Alistair and Ebony did.

"We found something!" Gibbon said giddily.

Alistair threw his claws up in the air. "We did, too! Let's see if Fiona and Declan found any clues!"

Eagerly, they opened the door to the house, where they found Fiona pretending to sip away at a bowl of tea. It was a funny sight, Gibbon had to admit. The bowl was at least half her size, but she clearly had the strength to hold it up.

Note to self, don't make Fiona mad. She might be small, but she is mighty!

"You guys are back!" Fiona said happily as she flew off the couch. "Did you find anything?"

"We found a piece of Declan's gold in the lake," Gibbon said triumphantly as he held out the coin.

"That *is* my gold!" Declan called out. He rushed over and held it next to his head with a huge smile. "See? Looks just like me!"

Gibbon laughed. When Declan smiled like that, he did look just like the portrait on the piece of gold.

"And we found your pot! It was empty just like you said," Ebony said.

"But there was water inside of it and these plants," Alistair added, holding out his claws so everyone could see the seaweed-like plants.

"Water?" Fiona hummed. She glanced at Declan and asked, "It hasn't rained in two weeks, right?"

"That's right," Declan said. "Believe me, I'd know if it had."

"Two weeks is enough time for the water to have dried up by now," Ebony said. "That means the water is from something else. From something recent."

"Was the pot next to a lake or something?" Fiona asked.

"Yes, it was," Ebony replied. "There was a piece of his gold near it, too."

Gibbon had heard about people having lightbulb moments—when an idea clearly struck them and a lightbulb went off in their head—but this was the first time he ever saw it. Fiona's bright green eyes got even brighter somehow.

"So Yuri and Gibbon found some gold in the lake, and Alistair and Ebony found Declan's pot with lake plants in it. That's it! I think I know what happened! Back to the lake!" Fiona said.

When they got to the lake, Fiona, without saying a word to her friends, dove into the water—surprising everybody.

"Can she swim?" Gibbon asked nervously.

"I think so?" Ebony replied, but her voice didn't sound very certain.

"She's been down there a while. . . ." Yuri mumbled a bit anxiously.

Just as Gibbon was really starting to worry, Fiona emerged from the water with . . . a horse? Gibbon blinked hard a few times, making sure he was really seeing what he thought he was.

The horse trotted out of the water as Fiona flew over to the others. She stopped next to Gibbon and shook herself like a dog, splashing water all over him.

"Hey!"

"Sorry," Fiona laughed.

"What's a horse doing in the lake?" Yuri scratched his head as he looked the blue and green horse up and down.

"Oh, I know!" Ebony jumped with excitement. "You're a kelpie! They're a type of creature that lives in lakes—but wait, what are you doing in Ireland? Aren't kelpies from Scotland?"

"During the last storm, I got washed away from my family's loch," the kelpie said sadly. "The waves were so rough. When I finally woke up, I found myself near the shore here, far from home. I went to the first lake I could find. I couldn't find my way back, so I just stayed here."

"What's this have to do with my gold?" Declan asked, rubbing his beard.

"I figured it out from your clues," Fiona said, grinning. "You guys found a piece of Declan's gold in the lake. And then you two found the pot and the lake plants inside it, which got me thinking—what if the gold was *inside* the lake? But just too deep for anyone to see it? What if something inside the lake took it? There's tons of lore about lake creatures in these parts."

"Awesome job, Fiona!" Yuri pumped his fist in the air.

"You guys were the ones to find all the clues. I just put them together," she said with a smile and a shrug. She turned toward the kelpie. "What's your name? And why did you take Declan's gold?"

"My name is Lachlan, and I'm sorry," the kelpie said, lowering his head. "Back home, we have beautiful rocks and fish all around us. But this lake is dark and dreary. I thought that your gold was pretty and shiny, and could make the lake feel more like home. I didn't realize it belonged to someone."

Declan watched Lachlan for a long moment. Then, he walked over to the kelpie and smiled at him.

"Don't worry, friend," Declan said. "No harm done here. I'm sorry you got washed away from your family. That storm almost ruined my house, too. Everyone needs their home." Declan and Lachlan exchanged friendly, understanding smiles.

"I have an idea!" Yuri said as a grin grew wide across his face.

CHAPTER EIGHT

OVER AND OUT

The sea shimmered brightly as the sun set, turning the water a beautiful shade of orange and pink. *What a great day!* Yuri thought to himself.

He was proud of what he and his friends had accomplished. Declan stood near them, smiling as he watched his new friend, Lachlan the kelpie, run toward his loved ones. His family was a rainbow of colors as they waited for him on the far shore.

Yuri was good with maps. Always had been. He planned the route from Scotland to Ireland and back again easily, and Fiona then flew to Lachlan's loch in Scotland and led his family to their missing member.

We found Declan's gold AND reunited the kelpie family! Yuri wanted to shout to the whole world, but he kept it inside. This moment was for the kelpies to reunite.

"Well done, students," a voice said. Yuri turned to see Fitzgerald leaning against a nearby tree and smiling. "You solved not one case, but two. See how even the smallest details can be important?"

"We do," Gibbon said, nodding. "I'm really glad we were able to help Declan find his gold and also help the kelpie get home. I admit I thought this mission was a little . . . boring at first. But now I get it."

Alistair flapped his wings in excitement. "Can we have another mission, Fitzgerald? Please?"

Fitzgerald laughed. "You all have to get back to the academy, first. But since you did such a good job, I'll make sure to keep you all in mind the next time I hear about a mission."

Yuri looked at each of his friends. Gibbon and Alistair were laughing and goofing off. Fiona gave Ebony a thumbs-up. And for the first time in ages, Yuri saw that Ebony looked not only happy, but confident. He felt lucky to have each of them as a friend. Now that they were starting to believe in themselves, what mission *wouldn't* they be able to solve?

Isle of MISFITS

PRANK WARS!

BOOK 3

by JAMIE MAE   illustrated by FREYA HARTAS

CONTENTS

CHAPTER ONE

A BABA YAGA, A TROLL, A GHOUL, AND A GREMLIN GET A MISSION

"We just got the coolest mission ever!"

Gibbon stopped walking when he heard someone talking about missions. Gibbon and his friends went on their first mission to help another creature a month ago, and he couldn't wait to go on another one! Who else could have gotten a mission?

When he turned to look, he saw Lissa the baba yaga in the center of a group of classmates. Gibbon had just left his History of Cursed Jewels class with his friends. Even though they all stood on the steps of the school building, he seemed to be the only one who heard Lissa. Ebony, Fiona, and Yuri chatted about what they'd learned while Alistair nodded along.

Gibbon stepped a little closer to Lissa to hear what she was saying better.

"What do you get to do?" a harpy asked, flapping her wings around excitedly.

"It's top secret," Lissa said as she folded her arms and grinned.

"Fitzgerald said he couldn't trust anyone else with this!" added Gashsnarl the ghoul with a high five to Trom.

Gibbon rolled his eyes. Maybe they were telling the truth, but he remembered how their team acted during the obstacle course race a few months ago. Gibbon's team came in second place in the competition, but still won because Fitzgerald saw Lissa trip Gibbon at the very end. If they were playing fair and square, Gibbon was sure he and his friends would have won.

Why would Fitzgerald give them a secret mission? Gibbon wondered. So what if Lissa and Gashsnarl were some of the top students in their class, coming second only to Ebony? They were cheaters.

"What's wrong?" Yuri asked, nudging Gibbon.

"Lissa's bragging about a secret mission," he muttered.

Yuri frowned as he looked over at the crowd surrounding Gashsnarl and Lissa. "Really? They got a mission? How come we didn't get another mission?"

"We helped Declan not too long ago," Ebony said.

Gibbon looked to Yuri and knew his friend was thinking the exact same thing as him. Helping Declan the leprechaun find his gold had been *so* long ago. Since then, all they'd been doing was going to classes, classes, and more classes. He loved learning about so many new things, but he longed for the adventure of another mission, probably just as much as Yuri did.

Alistair sighed. "I do miss helping other creatures. Remember how happy Declan was when we found his gold? And when we helped Lachlan find his family? That was pretty cool."

"Lissa is just being a show-off, like always," Fiona said as she flapped her wings with attitude.

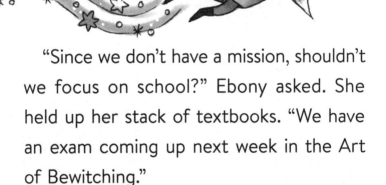

"Since we don't have a mission, shouldn't we focus on school?" Ebony asked. She held up her stack of textbooks. "We have an exam coming up next week in the Art of Bewitching."

Reluctantly, Gibbon nodded. His favorite part about being on the Isle of Misfits was all the books he got to read at the library. Their collection was so much bigger than the one at the castle he grew up in. His least favorite part of the Isle was tests, but with Ebony's help, he knew he'd usually pass them.

With one final look back at Lissa and Gashsnarl, Gibbon went with his friends to the ivy-covered library.

CHAPTER TWO

FITZ'S OFFICE

The next day, after classes were finished, Fitzgerald found Ebony and her friends and invited them into his office. Ebony was in awe over how organized Fitzgerald kept everything. Each book was alphabetized on his shelves by title and every piece of paper on his desk had a proper place. This was everything she dreamed her own dorm room would be, but Fiona was her roommate.

As much as she loved her fiery fairy friend . . . well, Fiona was a little tornado. All her quick flights around the room made papers go everywhere and she never, ever put books back in their proper place.

Gibbon plopped down in a chair in front of Fitzgerald's desk. Yuri and Alistair both sat down on a big couch, but Ebony and Fiona decided to stay standing—or in Fiona's case, flying.

"I have a mission for you," Fitzgerald said.

"A mission?!" Gibbon perked up in his chair.

"I knew it," Fiona said with a smirk. "What is it?"

"There's a cyclops who lives in the mountain on the other side of the island. Below the bridge leading to his cave, a pack of trolls have made themselves a home. The cyclops has been having problems with the trolls, and I'd like you to go and try to resolve them."

Ebony almost squealed with excitement. This was the very sort of mission she'd always wanted! She had aced her Conflicts & Conversations course last semester and would be able to use the skills she learned there to help the cyclops and the trolls.

As the team made their way to the other side of the island, everyone tried to guess what was wrong.

"The trolls are probably stinking up the whole mountain!" Gibbon said.

"I bet they are trying to make him solve a riddle every time he crosses the bridge," Yuri replied.

"Maybe they keep throwing parties and are being too noisy at night. Trolls aren't quiet," Alistair added.

"I bet the cyclops is the one causing trouble and we're the muscle Fitzgerald sent to make him behave himself!" Fiona said as she knocked her fists together.

Ebony laughed a little at that idea. She doubted that could be the case. She didn't try to guess during their journey to the other side of the island. There was no reason to—once they reached the cyclops, he'd tell them.

Instead, she enjoyed walking from the school buildings, past the wooden dorms with their garden-filled roofs, all the way across the training fields and beyond. A forest covered the north side of the island, and a mountain range was beyond that.

They walked through the forest and up one of the smaller mountains until they found the entrance to the cyclops's cave.

CHAPTER THREE

THE CYCLOPS'S CAVE

Alistair knocked on the side of the cave as Gibbon and Ebony wandered over to a little garden next to the entrance. Suddenly, they heard the thudding steps of something big coming toward them. Then, he was there.

Oh, wow! Fiona thought. The cyclops towered over them. And he was twice the size of Alistair! He was so tall that his head almost hit the ceiling. His whole body was squishy and his one, big eye looked over each of her friends until it stopped on her. *He's . . . he's so big!*

There were a lot of monsters at the academy bigger than Fiona, but not anything this big. She fluttered behind Ebony, glancing at the cyclops over her friend's shoulder.

He just has ONE eye, Fiona reminded herself. She had two good eyes. *I bet I can fly so fast, he won't see me!*

"Greetings! I'm Cyrus. Are you the group Fitz sent?" the cyclops asked.

"You mean Fitzgerald?" Ebony replied politely.

"Fitz and I go way back," Cyrus explained. "Come on in."

With his invitation, they entered the mysterious cave.

"This is so exciting," Ebony whispered to Fiona. "I've only ever read about a cyclops. I've never met one!"

"They're huge," Fiona muttered back.

"Whoa! This is so neat!" Alistair called out as he entered the living room. The furniture looked fancy, covered in royal purple velvet with gold patterns etched into the wood. Everything was perfectly placed, just like in Fitzgerald's office, which wasn't what Fiona was expecting at all. She thought a giant creature like a cyclops would have a messy home, not something that looked so . . . so nice.

"Can you tell us what's wrong?" Yuri asked. He barely looked around the home before getting straight to business. "Fitzgerald just said you had a problem with the trolls that live beneath the bridge near your cave."

"Yes," Cyrus said. "Oh, where are my manners? Would any of you like something to drink before I get started?"

The group happily accepted water after their long trek. When Cyrus went to the kitchen to get their drinks, Fiona darted around him quickly to find out whether he could see her. When he got out the glasses, she lingered on his right side, waving her hands to see if he would react. When he filled the glasses with water, she flew to his left side and made a funny face. Since he didn't seem to notice any of it, she guessed his vision wasn't that great. She trailed behind him as he walked back to the living room.

Fiona was the last one to get a glass of water when Cyrus passed them out. Once he handed her a tiny little cup, he smiled and said, "You are a quick little fairy, aren't you? Very energetic?"

She narrowed her eyes at him. "What do you mean?"

"All your flying around in the kitchen, making those faces and waving—did you think I didn't see you?"

Surprised, she almost dropped her glass. Okay, maybe his vision wasn't *that* bad.

"Thanks for the water," Alistair said. "Would you mind telling us about your trouble with the trolls?"

"Well, as you might have noticed, I don't have a door to my cave. There's a big boulder I can push in front of it, but that makes it hot inside and gives me no light during the day, so I keep it open. A month ago, I started to notice strange things happening.

One of my garden gnomes went missing. Then other small items around my home like books and slugs disappeared. Recently, it got worse. They started to play pranks on me. They . . ."

Cyrus's tan face turned a pinkish hue. "They . . . they put my underpants atop the mountain's flagpole. Then they loosened my salt shakers so when I used them, all the salt poured on top of my food and ruined it. And just yesterday, I found all the furniture in my bedroom upside down and stuck to the ceiling. Here, come and see for yourselves."

They put their drinks down on the table before following Cyrus further back into the cave. In the last room at the end of the hall, they each peeked in and saw exactly what he had described. His bed, along with his dresser, lamp, and a reading chair, were all stuck to the ceiling.

Gibbon suppressed a giggle, and Fiona whistled. "That's not easy to do."

"No, it isn't. Even for me, it'll take a while to get that stuff down." He rubbed his shoulder and frowned. "I slept on my couch last night. It wasn't very comfortable. After this last prank, I couldn't take it anymore, so I reached out to Fitz. Only the trolls could be doing this, I'm positive. So . . ." Cyrus turned back to them, a hopeful look in his eye. "Do you think you can help me?"

CHAPTER FOUR

TROLL TALK

Yuri thought the best way to handle this situation was by going to talk to the trolls. They all walked out of the cave and past the garden. Maybe they could talk some sense into the little tricksters and keep them from pulling any more pranks on Cyrus. On the walk down the mountainside, Ebony rambled on about all the things she learned in her Conflicts & Conversations course last semester. It was an advanced class, so of course, the only one in their group who had taken it so far was Ebony.

"Make sure to listen to both sides," Ebony said. "Don't accuse the trolls of anything. Be nice. Being mean won't get us anywhere, and it will just make them uncooperative."

"I've never met trolls before," Gibbon declared. "This will be so awesome!"

"Yes, you have," Fiona replied. "Remember Trom? The big, bald guy in Lissa's group? He's a troll."

Gibbon thought about it for a second. "Oh, yeah. You're right. I don't have any classes with him, so I never really see him."

"He's small for a troll," Fiona said. "I bet these bridge trolls are big!"

When they got closer to the bridge, Yuri had a feeling Fiona was right. They could feel the ground shaking and hear the sounds of laughter and music. Trolls, especially bridge trolls, were known for having fun. They liked to dance and listen to music, and they especially liked to trick people. So, these trolls playing pranks on their neighbor made sense to Yuri.

Before they got to the bridge though, another group crossed their path. Not just any group either, but Lissa, Gashsnarl, Trom, and their gremlin friend—Jori? Yuri was pretty sure that was the gremlin's name.

"Hey! What are you doing here?" Fiona asked as she flew up to be eye to eye with Lissa.

"We're on our mission," Lissa said proudly. "What are you guys doing here?"

"We're on a mission, too," Alistair said.

Lissa glanced over at Alistair before turning her attention to Gibbon. "Oh, yeah? What's your mission about?"

"Top. Secret." Gibbon grinned.

"That's not true," Ebony whispered. "Fitzgerald didn't say anything about—"

"You tell us about yours and we'll tell you about ours," Yuri interrupted.

Lissa thought this over for a second and exchanged a look with Gashsnarl. With a nod, Gashsnarl said, "We're helping some bridge trolls out. Their neighbor, a cyclops, has been stealing their stuff. He took some pots and pans from them. And lamps, too! It's even started to get worse. Now, he's playing pranks on them."

"What?" Ebony gasped.

"That's not true!" Fiona said. "Our mission is to help the cyclops because the bridge trolls are taking his things and playing pranks on *him*—not the other way around."

"Hey," Trom said, taking a step toward them. "My troll friends say they are the ones having things stolen! They're the ones telling the truth!"

"That's right, the trolls are innocent!" Lissa barked.

"No way, no how!" Fiona said crossing her arms.

"I saw the prank the trolls did myself," Gibbon argued.

"Well, I saw what the cyclops did to the trolls," Trom snapped.

"It doesn't matter what you guys say," Yuri said. "I know we'll get to the bottom of this and complete our mission."

Jori smirked. "No way. We'll finish our mission first."

CHAPTER FIVE

SPLITTING UP

"I have an idea," Alistair declared. His voice, though soft, was enough to stop the two groups from arguing. Slowly, each creature looked at Alistair.

"What's your idea, dragon?" Lissa asked.

"My name is Alistair," he said, annoyed.

Lissa should have known his name by now. "What if Gibbon and Ebony go with your team to help the trolls, and you and Trom come with Yuri, Fiona, and I to help the cyclops? You and Trom think the trolls are innocent, so you'll make sure we don't miss anything. And Gibbon and Ebony will make sure Gashsnarl and Jori don't miss anything, either."

Lissa watched Alistair carefully before looking to her friends. Jori and Gashsnarl looked at each other before shrugging, and Trom, with a huff, nodded. "Okay, we'll agree to that. But it'll only prove we're right and you're wrong."

"We'll see about that," Yuri said.

Alistair wasn't as sure as his friends were about what was true and what wasn't. If the trolls were having problems, they needed help, too. And at least this way, everyone would stop fighting and get towork to solve this problem.

Yuri, Fiona, Alistair, Lissa, and Trom all went back to see Cyrus. Trom and Yuri were silent on the way, both trying to be the leader of the new group. They walked faster than everyone else. Sometimes, Trom was ahead, and other times, Yuri.

"Boys," Lissa grumbled.

"For reals," Fiona said. The girls exchanged a look, then slowly smiled at each other and shook their heads.

Alistair was glad to see them agree on something, even if it was just on something small. Lissa and Fiona had always gotten into arguments at school. *Maybe this mission will change things,* he thought happily. Yuri and Trom kept racing to get to the cyclops's cave first, but Lissa and Fiona hadn't argued the whole time, so that was encouraging.

It was true Lissa cheated during the obstacle course challenge, but Alistair figured she'd learned her lesson. It had meant her team lost, so she probably wouldn't do it again. Besides, Lissa was like Ebony—at the top of their class. It was as important to her as it was to Ebony to stay that way. He could see how, even if it was wrong, Lissa might have thought it was a good idea at the time to trip Gibbon to stay on top.

As they walked through the garden outside of Cyrus's cave, Alistair paused to admire two shiny, red-capped gnomes that sat nicely between roses and daisies. He took a deep, deep breath—so deep that the colorful flowers swayed toward him. Sometimes, flowers smelled so good.

"Come on, Alistair!" Fiona called out as she entered the cave.

Quickly, he followed his friends.

"You're back!" Cyrus said.

"Hey, Cyrus! These are our classmates," Alistair explained, waving toward Lissa and Trom. "They heard the trolls' side of the story, and we thought it'd be good for them to hear your side, too."

"The trolls' side?" Cyrus frowned, looking directly at Trom. "Do you live under the bridge with them?"

Trom shook his head. "I live at the academy, not with the bridge trolls."

"Well, if Fitz sent you, then you must be okay," Cyrus said. "Did you see the bridge trolls on your way back here?"

"No, why?" Fiona asked with a tilt of her head.

"They stole more of my gnomes is why," Cyrus said with a lowered head. With a sigh, he led them back out to his garden and motioned to four patches in the ground where no grass had grown. "I used to have a whole pack of garden gnomes here, and now most of them are gone. What am I going to do?"

—— CHAPTER SIX ——

THE TROLLS UNDER THE BRIDGE

Gibbon and Ebony stuck together the whole way to the bridge. Gibbon wasn't sure what to think of Jori or Gashsnarl, or why Alistair thought this was a good idea. Their group of friends worked well together. They proved that during the obstacle course and when they found Declan's pot of gold, so why would Alistair want to mess that up by mixing the teams?

Jori was a hairy gremlin with bright green eyes. He kept glaring at Gibbon the whole way and it was freaking Gibbon out.

When they got to the bridge, it was the ghoul Gashsnarl who called down to the trolls. After a minute, the trolls stopped playing their music and stuck their heads up to see them.

"Gashsnarl!" one of the trolls called out with a smile. "Have you talked everything out with that cyclops?"

"Not yet," Gashsnarl grumbled. "These are our fellow students. They're looking into the same case we are—but they've already talked to the cyclops."

"Have you told him to return our pots and pans?" the troll asked. "We can't cook without them."

"We're hungry!" someone called out from below the bridge.

"We only have this one left," another troll said as he held up a small silver pan with a white handle. "Not nearly enough to cook food for everyone."

"We're also sick of him stealing our pants and setting them up on the bridge like flags!" another troll called out.

Gibbon frowned. "Well, maybe you shouldn't steal his underpants and hang them on the flagpole on top of the mountain."

The troll looked at Gibbon like he had said something awful. "Huh? We would never!"

"Have you also never gone into Cyrus's home and rearranged his furniture?" Ebony asked, but her tone was sweet and kind, so the troll didn't seem to take offense.

"We've never been inside his home. He's never invited us," the troll said.

"Not very friendly, that cyclops!" another troll called out.

"Told you so," Jori growled. "It's the cyclops, not the trolls."

"This is weird," Ebony said as she tapped her chin. "We should talk to Cyrus again. There seems to be more going on than we'd originally thought."

"Tell him to give us our pots back!" the troll said one last time before ducking back under the bridge.

When they made it back to the top of the mountain, the sky was turning all shades of orange and pink. They couldn't stay too long or else they wouldn't get back to the dorms before nightfall. Gibbon glanced at Ebony, who was looking up at the sky nervously. He knew she didn't like being out after dark.

"Night is the best, isn't it?" Gashsnarl said as he smiled up at the sky.

"Why do you say that?" Gibbon replied, even though he agreed. Back when he lived at the castle, Gibbon had to stay still during the day. It was only at night when he was free to move around and explore the area.

"Ghouls are night creatures," Gashsnarl said. "Aren't gargoyles, too?"

"Yeah, we are." Gibbon nodded.

"It's hard to adjust to the daytime schedule at school, isn't it?"

"It is. And I do miss running around in the moonlight," Gibbon said longingly.

"Same." Gashsnarl sighed as they arrived at the cave.

Ebony knocked on the wall. Not too long after, Cyrus came out wearing a robe and had soap on top of his head. He had a loofah in one hand and a rubber ducky in the other.

"Oops, we didn't mean to interrupt your shower," Ebony said.

"No worries, little griffin," Cyrus said. "You missed your friends. They were here about a half hour ago, looking over the damage the trolls did."

"Do you mind if we come in again, and show our classmates Gashsnarl and Jori what's been happening?" Ebony asked.

Cyrus looked at the two new creatures and nodded. He showed them to his bedroom, but while Jori and Gashsnarl went to look, Gibbon lingered in the kitchen. In the sink, he noticed a pile of pots and pans that hadn't been there when they visited Cyrus earlier.

Looking closer, he saw each pot and pan was silver and had white handles, just like the pan he had seen at the trolls' place.

"What's wrong?" Ebony asked as she walked over with Gashsnarl and Jori trailing behind.

"These are the pots and pans from the trolls, right?" Gibbon said as he pointed to the sink.

"Told you it was the cyclops!" Jori said.

"What?" Cyrus came out from the back room, scrubbing his head free of soap with a towel. When he saw the sink, he jumped from surprise. "What are all those pots doing in there?! I just cleaned!"

"These belong to the trolls." Gashsnarl folded his arms and looked at Cyrus sharply. "Explain yourself, cyclops!"

"I've never seen them before in my life," Cyrus said. He went to his shelves and motioned toward his pots. "Look! All of my pots are copper, not silver."

Gibbon looked at the two different types of pots, and then back at Gashsnarl. "What if he's telling the truth?"

Gashsnarl watched Gibbon carefully for a moment. "They can't both be telling the truth . . . can they?"

Ebony frowned and said, "Could it be that they're *both* being pranked?"

CHAPTER SEVEN

PRANK WARS!

After a good night's rest back at the academy, the two groups met again in front of the dorms. Lissa leaned against the wooden building, twirling her long, dark hair around a finger as Ebony told the group what they had discovered at Cyrus's home last night.

"So you think someone is pranking both of them?" Fiona asked.

"It could be, I guess," Lissa added.

"I think it's the only thing that makes sense, isn't it?" Yuri scratched his head, looking to his friends for answers.

"If both of them are the victims here, we should all work together," Alistair suggested.

Gashsnarl, Trom, and Jori looked at Lissa. Gibbon knew it all came down to her—if she said no, then that would be that. But to his surprise, she looked to Fiona and smiled.

"Okay, sure," Lissa said. "Let's all work together."

Gibbon's mouth almost fell open when he saw Fiona smile back at Lissa. *When did those two become friends?* he thought.

"But if they're both being pranked . . . then who's doing the pranking?" asked Yuri.

"Let's go back to the mountain and search for clues," Fiona said.

As one big team, they did just that. Trom and Yuri still jumped ahead to lead the group, but it seemed more like a game than an actual race. Each time Trom got the lead, he'd grin back at Yuri and dare him to catch up—only for Yuri to laugh and egg on Trom when he did.

Jori, Ebony, and Alistair all talked about their favorite class—Mischief and Mayhem: 101—while Lissa and Fiona joked about something Gibbon couldn't hear. Gashsnarl walked beside Gibbon, watching the two groups with a weird look on his face. Finally, he turned to Gibbon.

"Do you think this was what Fitzgerald had planned the whole time?" he asked.

Gibbon shrugged. "What do you mean?"

"We have never really gotten along. He didn't need to assign both of us to this mission. And he is the smartest guy on the whole island. He had to know the trolls and Cyrus were both being pranked. What if he assigned the two groups to make us all . . . become friends?"

Now that Gashsnarl said that, it did sound like something Fitzgerald would do. Gibbon looked at the group walking ahead of him, everyone talking and laughing with each other.

"Well, if that was Fitzgerald's plan, it looks like it worked," Gibbon said with a smile. Gashsnarl grinned and when he started to chuckle, Gibbon couldn't help but join in.

They wanted to check in with the trolls on their way up the mountain, but it was still too early for them.

"Bridge trolls like to stay up late and sleep until at least noon," Trom explained.

So instead of waiting for them, the group kept going all the way up to Cyrus's cave. It was still pretty early, but Gibbon hoped he would be awake. However, when they arrived, the boulder still blocked the entrance. Yuri knocked, but the cyclops didn't answer.

They waited outside in his garden. *This isn't good! We're on our second day and we have no leads and no one to talk to . . . can we even solve this?* Gibbon worried.

"Hey," Ebony called out and waved the group over to join her. She pointed to the shiny, red-capped gnomes near the daisies and roses. "The gnomes are back."

"I don't get it. Why would someone steal garden gnomes?" Trom asked.

Ebony pulled out her notepad from her backpack and flipped through her notes. "Yep, just as I thought. There were only two in the garden yesterday. Four were missing."

"Why would someone bring them back?" Yuri asked.

Gibbon got closer. He looked the gnomes over, one by one, before breaking out into a big smile. Back at the castle, he had to stay still all day while people walked by below. He knew just what it looked like to try to do that. And these gnomes? They weren't garden gnomes. He was pretty sure they were real gnomes pretending to be as still as garden gnomes!

He bent down low to get on eye level with the gnomes and locked eyes with the one closest to him. The very hardest part about staying still all day was not blinking. Staring contests were the only game the other gargoyles would play at the castle, so Gibbon was a champ. This gnome didn't stand a chance!

Squatting down was starting to feel like hard work. Gibbon could feel his legs start to cramp and shake, but he stayed focused on the gnome's eyes. He didn't want to miss the gnome blinking, except . . . it was taking an awfully long time, wasn't it? Maybe they really were just garden gnomes, but then who was playing the pranks? Just as Gibbon really started doubting himself, the gnome squinted.

"Ah!" the gnome shouted in a high-pitched voice, closing his eyes and rubbing them with his tiny hands. "No fair, no fair!"

"They're alive!" Jori shrieked, jumping into Alistair's arms.

"We've been discovered! RUN!" cried out another gnome. The six gnomes scattered, but Lissa and Gashsnarl each snatched one up, while Yuri and Ebony quickly grabbed the other four.

"Oh no, you don't!" Lissa said, lifting her captured gnome off the ground.

"Gnomes are really mischievous creatures," Ebony explained. "Were you the ones causing all the trouble for everyone?"

"Not trouble," one of the gnomes said. "We were only having a bit of fun!"

"Not anymore!" Lissa said as she held the gnome up to her face. "Got it? It's not funny. The trolls and the cyclops are really upset with each other."

"It was just a game," a gnome muttered.

"Your game caused a lot of problems," Ebony said.

"Is that fun for you?" Alistair asked.

Each of the gnomes frowned and hung their head.

"We're sorry," one of the gnomes said. "We didn't mean for it to make anyone angry. We just wanted to play!"

"If that's what you wanted, all you had to do was ask," Trom said, shaking his head with a grin. "Trolls love games. We'll introduce you to them and Cyrus, so you can say you're sorry. You can ask them to play with you, and I think you just might get some new friends. How's that sound?"

The gnomes looked at each other and smiled.

"You've got yourself a deal!" said the tiniest gnome.

CHAPTER EIGHT

THE FEAST

Lissa and Trom carried the trolls' pots and pans down to the bridge with Fiona. They could hear music before they even saw the bridge.

"Hey, everyone!" Trom called out once they arrived.

"Our pots!" a troll replied.

"We figured out what was going on," Fiona said as Lissa and Trom gave the trolls their items back. "Turns out, Cyrus's garden gnomes were real gnomes and they were the ones pulling the pranks."

"Ah, gnomes," the troll said. "They're little troublemakers!"

"Apparently, they thought they were playing and didn't mean to upset anyone," Lissa explained.

"We have our pots back and no harm was done, so all is forgiven," the troll said.

"Cyrus wanted us to invite you to his cave for dinner. What do you say?" Fiona asked.

More of the trolls appeared from under the bridge. "Food? We'd love to!"

Gibbon and the rest of the members of the two teams were already at the cave, helping Cyrus prepare for dinner when Fitzgerald arrived. Not too long afterward, Fiona, Lissa, Trom, and the bridge trolls came barreling in.

Cyrus had a long dining table that fit everyone. Even the gnomes ended up joining the meal. Everyone was scattered around the table, gnomes and trolls and a cyclops and Fitzgerald and friends, all talking and joking together.

To Gibbon's surprise, Cyrus was a great cook. He made a huge amount of food—meats, swamp stew, buttery mashed potatoes, moss pie, and even freshly baked bread! When the gnomes were served a worm potpie, Gibbon gagged and had to look away.

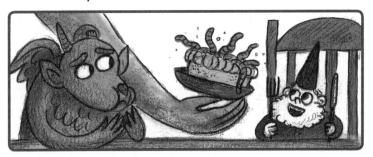

"You have a very nice place," one of the trolls said.

"Thank you," Cyrus replied. "I should have invited you all a long time ago. I'm sorry for all this mess."

"We are, too," the troll said.

"By the way, how did you manage to get Cyrus's furniture stuck to the ceiling?" Yuri asked the gnomes. "It's a good deal bigger than all of you."

"Ah, our finest prank," said a gnome. "All it took was a little bit of teamwork!" Everyone looked at each other and laughed.

Fitzgerald smiled as he watched everyone become friends before turning his attention to his students. "I'm glad to see you all managed to get along and solve this—together."

"I guess they're not that bad," Fiona said as she grinned at Lissa.

"Yeah, I guess so, too," Lissa replied.

Gibbon grinned as everyone began to dig into their food. He loved going on adventures, but this was the very best feeling—sitting at a table with new friends after completing another mission.

BOOK 4

Isle of MISFITS
THE CANDY CANE CULPRIT

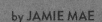

by JAMIE MAE   illustrated by FREYA HARTAS

CONTENTS

CHAPTER ONE

THE LEGEND OF SANTA

"It's nearing that time of year again!" Mrs. Masry declared cheerfully.

Gibbon perked up at his desk and focused on his teacher, Mrs. Masry. She was a sphinx with the head of a human and the body of lion, so it was hard to miss her as she walked around the room.

"Since Christmas is around the corner, I thought today's lesson should be on creatures and mythology surrounding the holiday." She clicked her slider and an image of an old lady on a broomstick appeared. "In Italy, this is called *La Befana*. Much like Santa Claus, she flies around rewarding good children with gifts and candy, while bad children get coal. Though humans might not believe so, *La Befana* is not really different from a normal witch. This was just something she did to help Santa out before people started noticing her flying around on a broomstick and panicked!"

With another click, her slider changed to reveal a big, hairy creature with wicked horns. Gibbon cringed—whatever that creature was looked so mean, he never wanted to meet one.

"This is a much more well-known creature from Germany, the Krampus. To date, a Krampus has not been found, but legend has it—"

The door to the classroom opened, cutting Mrs. Masry off.

Fitzgerald poked his head into the room. "Hello, Mrs. Masry. Would it be alright with you if I borrowed Gibbon and Alistair?"

"Of course!" Mrs. Masry replied brightly. "Go ahead, boys."

Alistair and Gibbon glanced at each other nervously as they got up. Gibbon didn't think they'd done anything wrong lately.

Ebony, Yuri, and Fiona were already in the hallway. When Gibbon saw them, excitement built up in his chest like a burst of bats. This wasn't about being in trouble, this was about a mission!

"What's going on? I'm missing class!" Ebony said anxiously.

"Your team has been making quite a stir lately," Fitzgerald began. "Declan and Cyrus were very pleased with your work and talked you up to all their friends. Word got around, and a very special someone has requested your help."

"Really?" Fiona said with wide eyes.

"Yeah!" Yuri cheered, high-fiving Alistair—or at least, he tried. Alistair missed Yuri's hand and almost fell forward, but Yuri caught him so he didn't hit the ground.

"Who?" Gibbon asked.

"This is a very high priority, very top secret mission," Fitzgerald whispered as he looked around the hallway. "I can't talk about the specifics here. Word cannot get out about this trouble, or it would cause a panic."

A panic? Top secret mission? A very important someone requesting their help? Gibbon bounced with excitement. This mission was going to be something special!

"I brought you some essentials for this mission. Be sure to bundle up!" Fitzgerald picked up a box from alongside the wall and put it down in front of them.

Gibbon rushed to open the box first. With a raised eyebrow, he pulled out a fluffy sweater with a big, glittery Christmas tree. A bell hung off the sweater at the top of the tree, so it jingled every time it moved.

"We have to wear this?" Yuri asked, taking the sweater from Gibbon.

"It's going to be cold where you're going," Fitzgerald said. "Chop, chop. The quicker you layer up, the quicker we can leave."

Yuri put on the jingly sweater as Fiona pulled out a tiny pair of red-checkered mittens and matching earmuffs. Ebony picked out a green, fluffy hat to protect her ears and a matching scarf. Alistair grabbed the other big sweater, which was decorated with a cat popping out of a present as it ate a gingerbread man. When he pulled it over his head, the pointed scales on his back poked through the fabric. His claws tore the tips of his mittens, too.

Gibbon grabbed the last item, a puffy, oversized candy cane-decorated jacket.

Fitzgerald chuckled and said, "Let's go!"

CHAPTER TWO

A VERY SPECIAL VIP

An icy wilderness greeted them when they landed. Even Fitzgerald shivered in the chilly wind. In the distance, they could see mountains made of nothing but snow and ice. Behind the big wall of ice in front of them, Alistair could see a warm and welcoming glow. But he couldn't figure out what it could possibly be.

Who would they be able to help in a deserted winter wonderland like this? Fiona huddled close to Ebony as both friends' teeth chattered. Yuri seemed perfectly okay, happy even. Alistair wondered if this was the sort of place Yuri used to call home.

"Can we get somewhere warm, *please*? Fairies aren't meant to be this cold!" Fiona said, shivering.

"It shouldn't be much longer," Fitzgerald replied as he searched the sky.

As soon as Alistair took a step forward, he slid on the ice and waved his arms around to try to catch his balance. His clawed feet almost made it seem like he was on ice skates, but there were too many blades to stay stable. Ebony grabbed ahold of his arm and helped him stay upright— just as something zoomed over their heads.

Ebony jumped in surprise as she looked up to see what it was. The sun gleamed so bright in the sky, all she could make out was the creature's outline. What was it? A Pegasus? Hippogriff? No, it didn't look like either of those things—there was more than one flying creature and they were . . . pulling a sleigh?

"Santa!" Fiona shouted with delight. "Hey! It's *Santa*!"

"No way!" insisted Gibbon.

Alistair couldn't believe it! The sleigh circled above before coming down to land right next to them. It kicked up a little snow as it did, but Alistair didn't care. His mouth hung wide open as he watched a big, jolly man in a red suit with a white beard step out of the sleigh.

There was no doubt. It was Santa.

"Ho, ho, ho! Hello, there," Santa greeted them. "You must be the team I've heard so much about! I'm Santa Claus, though some call me Kris Kringle. You can call me Kris. These are my good friends: Dasher, Dancer, Prancer, Vixen, Comet, Cupid, Donner, Blitzen and . . . does he really need any introduction?"

Santa laughed as he patted the lead reindeer on the head, who smiled and raised his red, glowing nose higher.

Santa! Alistair still couldn't believe it. Not just Santa, but Santa *and* his reindeer!

"Fitz, always good to see you." Santa reached out his hand and shook Fitzgerald's.

"Always happy to come visit," Fitzgerald replied.

"Now, let me show you around my workshop." Santa reached into his sleigh and pressed a button. With a shudder, the ice wall opened up to reveal a sprawling village behind it. Alistair realized this was what created the warm glow they had been seeing—a whole town was hidden behind the ice wall! Once they all stepped inside, the cold melted away—like magic!

Alistair could hear Fiona sigh with relief
as she tilted her face toward the glow.

"These are the elves' homes," he explained as they walked past cabins covered in Christmas lights. Elves walked along the icy streets, chatting and nodding hello as they passed by. Some carried grocery bags while others carried tools as they went off to work. At the very center of town was the biggest building of all—a huge factory.

"And here is my factory where all the toys are made." Santa opened a door to the building and let them in. "We only have this one doorway in and out, and all the windows are sealed shut. It helps keep the environment perfect for the elves to paint and craft toys."

"We are so—" Ebony stopped, stumbling over her words as she turned to look up at Santa. "So honored you asked us to help you, Santa, sir!"

"No sirs needed, we're all friends here! You came highly recommended by my good friend Declan. I'm sure you're all wondering why you're here, and I'm afraid to say it's because . . ." For the first time, it looked like Santa's good cheer left him. He frowned as he looked around his factory.

"We've been having a lot of trouble with vandalism in my factory. Worse than just that, toys are being *destroyed*. For the first time ever, we're awfully behind schedule and I'm afraid if we can't get this under control soon . . . we might not have enough toys come Christmas."

CHAPTER THREE

THE MONSTER IN THE MOUNTAINS

*N*ot enough toys for Christmas?!

Gibbon couldn't believe it. Could there be anything worse than that? One Christmas back at the castle, Gibbon had found a lump of coal near the gargoyles' Christmas tree. Surely, it hadn't been meant for him . . . but he never did find out *who* the coal was left for, either. Still, he remembered that crushing moment he saw the coal and thought he wasn't going to get a present. Thankfully, he'd found a wrapped package addressed to him moments afterward.

"Also, *a lot* of candy canes have gone missing, along with some coal," Santa said as he looked down at Gibbon.

Gibbon squirmed and looked away. Thankfully, some elves scurried over to join them.

"We know who the culprit is!" one of the elves said.

Another nodded. "It's the monster of the mountains!"

"Shhh, we shouldn't talk about it," a third elf whispered. "If you talk about it, it will hear you and come for us."

"Oh, hogwash." Santa shook his head. "My elves believe there's some monster that comes down from the mountain and lurks around the North Pole at night. But no one has ever seen it."

"But, Santa!" the elf squeaked. "Even the reindeer are scared!"

"They're always a little anxious around Christmas," a woman said as she walked over to them. She had curly white hair and wore a red dress that matched Santa's suit.

Santa smiled brightly. "Everyone, I would like to introduce you to my wife, Mrs. Claus."

"Fitzgerald! It's been too long," Mrs. Claus declared as she gave the large gargoyle a quick hug. "How about we catch up over a nice cup of hot cocoa and let your students get to work?"

"I'll be around if you need me," Fitzgerald said to the group before following Mrs. Claus across the factory floor.

Once they were gone, Ebony asked, "What do you think is going on here, Santa?"

"I'm not sure, but I do know it's *not* any of my elves. And the ice wall you saw out front circles the whole village. Only the head elf, Mrs. Claus, and myself can open and close the gate, so I don't know how anything could have gotten in."

"A monster sounds pretty bad," Gibbon whispered to Alistair, who nodded in reply.

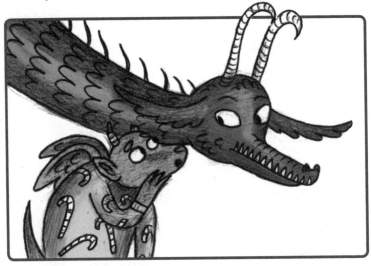

"Psh, I could take it on," Fiona said, throwing punches at an imaginary opponent. "I'll protect you boys, don't worry!"

Santa laughed and waved them along. They walked through the factory where elves were rushing around an assembly line building toys piece by piece. At the very end, an elf grabbed the finished toy and wrapped it up so fast, it made Gibbon stop in awe.

"Come along now," Santa called as he went into the next room. Gibbon rushed to catch up. When he got into the room, his heart jumped in his chest at the sight before him—a room made entirely of candy canes!

The walls were made of it; even the furniture and the pictures were made out of it. It was everywhere!

"You can use this as your headquarters, team," Santa said.

"Kris! We need you out here!" An elf shouted.

"I'll be back in a moment," Santa told them.

After he left, Gibbon walked up to one of the candy cane chairs like he was in a trance. He couldn't hear his friends talking. Every one of his senses was taken up by the candy cane. The delicious, sweet, peppermint-y *candy cane*.

Just one bite, Gibbon thought. It couldn't do any harm if he took just one little, itty, bitty nibble, right? He leaned close to the chair and bit the back of it, sighing with delight at the taste. *Maybe one more . . .*

Before he knew what he was doing, he took one bite, two bites, three, and then more and more!

Once he realized what he'd done, Gibbon covered his mouth with both hands and looked around. His friends gaped at him, their mouths open wide in horror. *Oh, no! I completely ate one of Santa's chairs!*

That had to be naughty-list material!

Santa came back into the room and glanced around, frowning at the area where the chair used to be. "Hmm . . . it looks like even *more* canes are missing now."

THE STAKEOUT

Their first night at the factory, the misfits decided to have a stakeout. If the elves were right and there was a monster breaking into the factory, they thought this was the best way to prove it—and maybe even catch it.

Ebony and Yuri were on the east side of the factory, hiding behind some boxes. Alistair and Gibbon were on the west side, crouching beside the present-wrapping table. Since Fiona was the smallest—and the stealthiest—she was flying around in case something showed up.

Fiona wasn't scared one bit. She might be tiny, but she was sure she could take on the creature, no matter its size. She was, however, tired when it finally struck midnight and there was no sign of anything. She sat on top of a table, just about to doze off, when a *CRASH!* came from the south side of the factory. Fiona flew over to Ebony and Yuri, since they were closest to the sound.

"What was that?" Ebony whispered.

"I don't know, we should go check it out," Yuri said.

Then something else shattered right near where the crashing noise came from.

On the other side of the factory, Fiona could see Alistair's shadowy figure ducking beneath the table, barely fitting under it. Gibbon dove down right beside Alistair, covering his head with his hands.

Fiona and Ebony exchanged a look before shaking their heads and following Yuri to the other side of the factory. They were careful not to make any loud sounds themselves. But when they finally got there, all they found were tipped-over boxes and a few broken toys.

"Snow," Yuri whispered as he knelt down and pointed to a half-melted puddle on the ground. Once they picked up the boxes, they found more melting snow underneath. They followed the trail through the factory until they came to where Alistair and Gibbon were hiding. The pair was shaking and holding each other tight.

"Oh, stop being such scaredy-cats," Fiona sighed.

"W-we saw it," Alistair stuttered.

"It ran right by the table!" Gibbon declared. "It was *huge* and had furry feet."

Another *CRASH!* came from somewhere else in the factory. Fiona darted toward the door, since that was the only way for the monster to get out. As she flew, she saw more damaged toys and small chunks of broken candy cane. When she made it to the front door, it was already wide open with no one in sight.

It got away!

CHAPTER FIVE

HOW THE TOYS GET MADE

"I'm just saying, the more candy cane the monster steals, the less candy cane there'll be for everyone else. It's tragic!" Gibbon said with a frown.

"Shouldn't we be more focused on all the toys that were broken last night?" Fiona huffed.

"That's sad, too," Gibbon replied. "But the candy cane . . ."

Alistair patted his friend on the shoulder. Living with Gibbon had taught him a lot about the little gargoyle, including the fact that Gibbon had a mighty strong sweet tooth. "It's okay, buddy. We'll save the toys *and* the candy cane!"

"I think we should split up," Ebony suggested. "Alistair, why don't you stay behind and gather more information about the monster from the elves? Yuri and Fiona, go check the ice mountain and see if you can find anything there. Gibbon, we can search around the North Pole for any way the monster might have gotten past the ice wall."

"Do I have to search outside . . . *where the monster is?*" Gibbon pouted.

"Come on," Ebony urged him as she took his hand.

Alistair was happy to stay in the warm factory and talk with all the elves. Once his friends left, he went from workshop to workshop asking what anyone knew about it. Most were too scared to talk about it until he met Millicent, the head elf. She worked at the very start of the assembly line.

"Oh, *that* monster," Millicent muttered. "It causes us so much trouble!"

"I'm really sorry about that," Alistair said.

"Santa said you'll fix it, and Santa's never wrong," she replied with a curt nod. She paused and looked Alistair over head to toe. "You know, a big guy like you could probably get a *lot* of toys done," she hummed.

"You think so?"

"Wanna give us a hand while you ask your questions?"

"Yes!" Alistair had never made toys before, but he *did* love toys, so he was sure he'd really enjoy making them.

"Okay, here's a set of tools for you." Millicent opened up a box filled with teensy hammers and wrenches and a bunch of other things Alistair didn't know the names of. He swallowed hard. The tools were all so . . . tiny.

His hands? Not so tiny.

"That toy is mostly done," Millicent said as she pointed to a rocking horse. "Could you please bring it over? It usually takes three elves to move those."

Alistair nodded, and it was easy enough. To him, the horse was light and he made sure to take extra care watching his steps as he made his way back to Millicent.

"What do you think the monster is?" Alistair asked as he set the toy down.

"Some say he's the Krampus," Millicent replied. "He's supposed to be a mix between a monster and a man, and very mean. He's the opposite of Santa. It would make sense. We're creating the toys. And he's destroying them."

Alistair nodded as she spoke. *Wasn't Mrs. Masry talking about the Krampus before we left school? She said it's never been found.*

"Now, take the hammer and bang in those nails that are sticking out," Millicent instructed.

Alistair grabbed the horse's head and tried to hit the nails with the tiny hammer, but it was awkward to hold, so he kept missing. As he leaned against the rocking horse trying, trying, and trying again to get those nails  pushed in, he heard a *CRACK!* Jumping away from it, he saw the neck of the horse was dangling forward now.

"I'm sorry!"

"It's okay, we all make mistakes," Millicent said. "Let's give it another go with something else . . . how about that toy robot? Take the screwdriver and finish twisting in the bolts on its back, okay?"

"Santa told us that you're one of the only people who can open the ice wall's gate. Have you seen anything strange near that area whenever you've used it?" Alistair asked as he looked around his box for the screwdriver.

"Nothing that I've ever noticed. It's hard to believe whatever it is would have slipped in that way," Millicent answered as Alistair found the screwdriver. Delicately, he tried to hold it with his claws, but it was hard for him to maneuver. Frustrated, he held the robot a little tighter so it'd stay in place as he tried again when—*CRACK!*

He broke *another* toy. He groaned as he set it down.

"It's okay, it's okay!" Millicent said as she patted his arm. "You didn't mean to, you're a dragon, not an elf. This doesn't come naturally to you."

That made Alistair feel a little better. He was a dragon and this workshop was built for elves, so it made sense he didn't fit in that well.

Wait . . . what if the monster doesn't mean to break things, too? What if he's just too big to get around this tiny workshop like me?

"Why do you think it steals coal?"

Millicent frowned. "I have no idea! Who would *want* coal?"

Alistair stayed with Millicent a little longer, learning her toy-making ways before he started to wander around the workshop again.

He bumped into tables and stubbed his toe on tiny little stools, which made him trip and almost crash into a box of freshly wrapped toys.

The monster really could just be too big! This place is hard for me to walk around in.

Out of the corner of his eye, he saw

something wet on the floor. When he got closer to inspect it, it was clearly footprints leading out the back door, where even more footprints leading away from the building were easy to see in the snow.

Big footprints.

Too big for Santa and his elves or for Ebony and Gibbon.

CHAPTER SIX

THE NAUGHTY LIST

Ebony shivered as she and Gibbon walked along the ice wall. She couldn't see any way the monster might have been able to get in. Unless the monster could jump really high or maybe fly.

Once they reached the front door, something caught her attention in the snow. She squatted down and picked up a clump of white hair.

"Santa's?" Gibbon asked as he looked over the possible clue.

"This is more . . . fur-like than Santa's hair, don't you think?" Ebony replied.

Gibbon looked closer and nodded. He walked around searching for more, but every time he heard the jingle of reindeer bells or footsteps, he jumped.

"Why are you so anxious, Gibbon? You seemed scared of Santa back in the workshop, too."

Gibbon lowered his head and dug his toes into the snow. "Um, no reason . . ."

"Oh, come on. You can tell me. We're friends!"

Slowly, Gibbon looked up at her. His eyes darted around, making sure no one else was nearby, then he whispered, "I . . . I think I'm on the naughty list."

"You?" Ebony gasped. "I don't believe it. No way, no how."

Gibbon wasn't convinced. "Back at the castle, I could never sit still like I was supposed to, and I played pranks on people. Nothing too bad, mostly just dropping snowballs down on them or moving around into different poses to confuse people. But still . . . I wasn't supposed to do that stuff. It's why Fitzgerald brought me to the isle."

"But since you arrived, you've done nothing but help others. There's no way Santa has you on the naughty list."

Gibbon was about to smile when Alistair appeared around the corner. He was hunched over, looking closely at the ground and walking so fast, he was about to run into them!

"Alistair!" Ebony called out. He looked up and skidded to a stop, kicking up some snow on his friends.

"Oh, hi! What are you guys doing here?" Alistair asked.

"Looking for a way the monster might have gotten in. Look at what we

found," Ebony said as she held up the white fur. "I think it might be a clue. What are you doing here?"

"Following these," Alistair said, pointing down to the footprints. "They led me here."

"So they went through the village, and not along the wall," Ebony noted. That had to be why she and Gibbon hadn't noticed them yet.

"The footprints look like they go directly out the gate. We should follow them," Ebony said. She used the key Santa gave her to open the gate. Once they started following the footprints farther and farther away from the ice wall, they came across Yuri's as well.

Hmm, it's strange how much they look alike, Ebony thought.

Both sets of footprints were headed toward . . . the mountain!

"Yuri and Fiona went up the mountain, right?" Gibbon gulped.

"And the footprints are going that way, too," Alistair added.

"We have to warn them!" Ebony shouted.

CHAPTER SEVEN

UP IN THE MOUNTAINS

Yuri watched as Fiona shivered more and more the longer they were outside.

"It's too bad you don't have warm fur like me," he said.

"I am beautiful the way I am," Fiona said as she held her head up high. "I'm just not meant for c-cold we-weather."

She wrapped her arms tightly around herself, but almost flew backward when a strong gust of wind hit them. Yuri reached out and let her rest in his hand. She huffed, glaring at him like her poor, furless skin was his fault.

Fiona hummed as she looked him over. "Can I bundle up in your man bun to stay warm? That way, I don't have to worry about flying in this harsh, cold wind, too."

"Sure?" Yuri said a bit uneasily.

Fiona flew up to his head. He could feel her digging her way into his man bun and sighing contentedly once she was seated on his head. "Okay, maybe having fur isn't so bad."

Yuri laughed as they continued up the mountainside. He was built perfectly for this weather and for easily scaling mountains and conquering icy grounds, too. While he didn't come from the North Pole, his home wasn't all too different from here.

"This place is perfect," Yuri said. "If I wanted to, I could sneak around here so easily since I'm all white like the snow. Back home, my brothers and I always did that to play tricks on each other."

As soon as he said it, he realized what it could mean. If no one ever saw the monster during the day . . . maybe it wasn't because it *only* came out at night, but because it was white and blended into the snow, too.

Once they were halfway up the mountain, Fiona pointed out an alcove off to their left.

Yuri walked over to explore it. Inside was a camp with a firepit in the center, a couple crate boxes sitting around like chairs, a unicorn beanie bag, a big stack of picture books, and calendars scattered around that contained pictures of warm places. A book was left open next to the firepit called *How to Blend in With the Locals* that had highlight marks and sticky notes in it.

"Candy cane!" Fiona shouted.

Yuri squatted down and saw little pieces of it everywhere, right next to a comb with lots of white fur and gel caught in it.

"Hey, look over there. What's that?" Fiona asked, pointing to the far side of the camp. Yuri carefully stepped over the firepit and over to an old, brown sleigh filled with pillows and sheets with bunnies on them.

"Looks like someone's bed," Yuri said. But it was a very lumpy one, so Yuri moved the sheets to get a better look only to discover a whole pile of coal.

"Ah-ha! We found our culprit!" Fiona shimmied on his head in excitement.

"Maybe, but this doesn't look like the home of a monster," Yuri said as he glanced over the camp, catching sight of a big stuffed animal that looked well-used. It took Yuri a moment to realize it was a dog, and almost life-sized, too.

Then the sound of footsteps caught his attention. He turned around, seeing a long, dark shadow in the entrance of the alcove.

"It's the monster!" Fiona yelled. "Don't worry, Yuri, I'll protect you!"

The shadow turned into something a little bigger than Yuri, with just as much long, white hair that mostly covered its face. It was another yeti! He danced as he walked, giggling to himself as he held one fistful of candy canes in one hand and cradled a bunch of coal with his other.

Candy cane bits stuck to the fur that hung over his face, and the red of the candy had dyed his fur in other places, too.

Yep, they definitely found their culprit. Except, he wasn't a monster at all.

When the other yeti noticed them, he yelped and dropped everything like he was the one scared. "Wh-wh-who are you?!"

"We're helping Santa. He wanted to know what's been breaking into his factory, destroying toys, and stealing candy cane and coal. It seems like that creature is you!" Fiona said, pointing at the yeti. Instantly, she shivered and pulled her hand back into Yuri's warm fur.

Another shadow rounded the corner of the alcove right before Alistair appeared. He ran straight over to the other yeti, breathing heavily as he did.

"Yuri!" Alistair shouted. "Watch out! The monster is coming this way!"

Ebony and Gibbon rounded the corner next, each eyeing Alistair strangely before looking over to Yuri and Fiona.

"Uh . . . Alistair?" Yuri called out.

His dragon friend jumped as he turned around. "Yuri! Wait, how are you . . . ?" He glanced behind him at the other yeti, then back at Yuri, then back at the yeti again.

"*Ahhhh!*" Alistair stumbled away from the other yeti. After a few clumsy steps, he fell straight into a pile of snow.

"It's okay, Alistair. He's a yeti, like me, and *he's* the one that's been breaking into Santa's shop," Yuri explained. "I just don't know why yet."

The yeti sighed and hung his head low. "I'm sorry! I'm Gunderson. I only went into the workshop to get some coal for my fire. Even us yetis get cold at night."

"Why break all the toys?" Ebony asked.

"I didn't mean to! Everything is so small, and I'm not small at all! I always go when it's dark, because I don't want to scare the little elves. At night, I can barely see. Even during the day, it can be hard because of this long hair!"

"Here," Yuri said as he walked over to his fellow yeti. "Try this!"

Yuri always carried an extra hair tie on his wrist, and being an expert at this by now, he got all of Gunderson's hair up into a bun on the top of his head and tied it in place.

"Wow! Thank you. I can see so much better now!"

"What about the candy canes?" Gibbon asked.

"I know I *shouldn't* take them because they're not mine, but I can't help myself. They're just so delicious!" Gunderson replied nervously.

Gibbon nodded sympathetically. "Yeah, they *are* really good."

"With all the toys you broke, there might not be enough for all the kids at Christmas this year," Alistair said with a frown.

"No!" Gunderson roared, making the mountain shake. All of the misfits shrank back, surprised by the loud cry.

"I didn't mean for that to happen! Is there anything I can do to help Santa and the elves? Please, please, *please*?! I don't want to be the reason someone doesn't get their toys—or worse, their candy canes!"

"Let's go back to the factory and see if there's any way we can help Santa," Ebony suggested.

"Oh, man. Does this mean I'm on the naughty list now?" Gunderson asked, biting his nails.

CHAPTER EIGHT

SAVING CHRISTMAS

"**C**'mon, guys. We can do this!" Alistair declared as he held up some half-finished toys. "Millicent already taught me how, so I can show you guys, too!"

Ebony and Fiona grabbed their own boxes of tools and sat down next to Alistair. Both quickly caught on, especially Fiona since her tiny hands worked so well with the elves' tools. Yuri and Gunderson, like Alistair, were too big for the tools, but they helped the elves move the heavy bags of toys around the workshop and onto the sleigh.

Gibbon learned he had a knack for wrapping gifts, since his claws worked to not only cut the wrapping paper, but also make the ribbons all pretty and twisty! It took them all day and a lot of effort, but they were able to get all the toys finished.

"We did it!" Millicent cheered at the front of the factory. "We've made all the toys on our list!"

"Indeed, you all did a great job," Santa said, but his smile wasn't as big as Gibbon expected it to be.

"What's wrong?" Fiona asked.

"I'm afraid it still took longer than we expected. I'm hours behind schedule and I'm not sure if I'll be able to deliver all the toys in time. . . . That is, unless I can find someone to help me."

"Help?" Gibbon grinned and looked to his friends, each of them jumping with excitement. Did that mean . . . they could actually go out and deliver toys with Santa? Gibbon couldn't even imagine how cool it would be to ride in the sleigh, shimmy down chimneys, and leave toys under Christmas trees. And all the cookies he would get to eat, too!

"Fitzgerald!" Gibbon turned around to look at the bigger gargoyle, who was enjoying a nice cup of hot cocoa with Mrs. Claus nearby. "Can we? Can we please?"

Fitzgerald took a long sip of his cocoa before putting his mug down. "You've done a great job, so . . . I think you should finish what you started and see this mission through."

Everyone cheered. Ebony flapped her wings in joy while Yuri and Alistair high-fived—successfully this time! And Fiona did a little dance in the air.

Santa placed a red hat on top of Gibbon's head and grinned down at him. "You are all most certainly on my nice list this year."

Gibbon's heart felt like it could soar right out of his chest. He wasn't on the naughty list after all!

"Come along now, we don't have any time to waste!" Santa hopped onto his fully packed sleigh and patted the seat next to him. Giddily, Gibbon scurried into the sleigh and sat down next to Santa. Fiona sat on her friend's shoulder while Gunderson and Yuri made themselves nice and comfy right behind them.

As they took off into the snowy night sky, Ebony and Alistair flew right alongside them, claws clasped, smiling and laughing all the way.

JAMIE MAE is a children's book author living in Brooklyn with her fluffy dog, Boo. Before calling New York home, she lived in Quebec, Australia, and France. She loves learning about monsters, mysteries, and mythologies from all around the globe.

⟷

FREYA HARTAS is a UK-based illustrator specializing in children's books. She lives in the vibrant city of Bristol and works from her cozy, cluttered desk. Freya loves to conjure up humorous characters, animals, and monsters, and to create fantastical worlds and places for them to inhabit and get lost in.

ELLA AND OWEN

Dragon twins Ella and Owen are always at odds. Owen loves to lounge and read, but adventurous Ella is always looking for excitement. Join these hilarious siblings as they encounter crazy wizards, stinky fish monsters, knights in shining armor, a pumpkin king, and more!

THE ALIEN NEXT DOOR

Harris thinks there's something strange about the new kid at school, Zeke, and that's because Zeke is the new kid on the planet! As Harris looks for the truth, Zeke realizes that he has a lot to learn about Earth and blending in. Will Zeke be able to make friends, or will Harris discover his secret? Join their adventures that are out of this world.

Tales of SASHA

Meet Sasha, one very special horse who discovers she can fly! With the help of her best friend, Wyatt, Sasha sets out to find other flying horses like her. Come along on their adventures as they explore new places and make new friends.

Mighty MEG

Meg's life is turned upside down when a magical ring gives her superpowers! But Meg isn't the only one who changes. Strange things start happening in her once-normal town. Can Meg master her new powers and find the courage to be the hero her town needs?